A CHRISTMAS
Classic

A CHRISTMAS
Classic

Augsburg
MINNEAPOLIS

TABLE OF *Contents*

Compiled and Designed by
Leonard Flachman and Karen Walhof

In many homes it is a Christmas Eve custom to read from St. Luke and St. Matthew.

THE CHRISTMAS
Gospel

In those days a decree went out from Emperor Augustus that all the world should be registered. This was the first registration and was taken while Quirinius was governor of Syria. All went to their own towns to be registered. Joseph also went from the town of Nazareth in Galilee to Judea, to the city of David called Bethlehem, because he was descended from the house and family of David. He went to be registered with Mary, to whom he was engaged and who was expecting a child.

While they were there, the time came for her to deliver her child. And she gave birth to her firstborn son and wrapped him in bands of cloth, and laid him in a manger, because there was no place for them in the inn.

In that region there were shepherds living in the fields, keeping watch over their flock by night. Then an angel of the Lord stood before them, and the glory of the Lord shone around them, and they were terrified. But the angel said to them, "Do not be afraid; for see—I am bringing you good news of great joy for all the people: To you is born this day in the city of David a Savior, who is the Messiah, the Lord. This will be a sign for you: you will find a child wrapped in bands of cloth and lying in a manger." And suddenly there was with the angel a multitude of the heavenly host, praising God and saying,

"Glory to God in the highest heaven,
and on earth peace
among those whom he favors!"

When the angels had left them and gone into heaven, the shepherds said to one another, "Let us go now to Bethlehem and see this thing that has taken place, which the Lord has made known to us." They went with haste and found Mary and Joseph, and the child lying in the manger. When they saw this, they made known what had been told them about this child; and all who heard it were amazed at what the shepherds told them. But Mary treasured all these words and pondered them in her heart. The shepherds returned, glorifying and praising God for all they had heard and seen, as it had been told them.

In the time of King Herod, after Jesus was born in Bethlehem of Judea, wise men from the East came to Jerusalem, asking, "Where is the child who has been born king of the Jews? For we observed his star at its rising, and have come to pay him homage."

When King Herod heard this, he was frightened, and all Jerusalem with him; and calling together all the chief priests and scribes of the people, he inquired of them where the Messiah was to be born. They told him, "In Bethlehem of Judea; for so it has been written by the prophet:

'And you, Bethlehem,
in the land of Judah,
are by no means least
among the rulers of Judah;
for from you shall come a ruler
who is to shepherd my people Israel.'"

Then Herod secretly called for the wise men and learned from them the exact time when the star had appeared. Then he sent them to Bethlehem, saying, "Go and search diligently for the child; and when you have found him, bring me word so that I may also go and pay him homage." When they had heard the king, they set out; and there, ahead of them, went the star that they had seen at its rising, until it stopped over the place where the child was. When they saw that the star had stopped, they were overwhelmed with joy. Entering the house, they saw the child with Mary his mother; and they knelt down and paid him homage. Then, opening their treasure chests, they offered him gifts of gold, frankincense, and myrrh. And having been warned in a dream not to return to Herod, they left for their own country by another road.

Now after they had left, an angel of the Lord appeared to Joseph in a dream and said, "Get up, take the child and his mother, and flee to Egypt, and remain there until I tell you; for Herod is about to search for the child, to destroy him."

Then Joseph got up, took the child and his mother by night, and went to Egypt, and remained there until the death of Herod. This was to fulfill what had been spoken by the Lord through the prophet, "Out of Egypt I have called my son."

When Herod died, an angel of the Lord suddenly appeared in a dream to Joseph in Egypt and said, "Get up, take the child and his mother, and go to the land of Israel, for those who were seeking the child's life are dead."

Then Joseph got up, took the child and his mother and went to the land of Israel.

Where does the story of Jesus begin? With Bethlehem? With the announcement by the angel Gabriel to Mary? With the angel's appearance to Zechariah, telling him that he would yet father a son who will go before the Lord "in the spirit and power of Elijah"? Or does the story start far back in the dim beginnings when, after man's fall into sin, God told Satan that the seed of woman would bruise his head? The promise of a Messiah or Savior was repeated many times through the centuries, and the people of Israel lived in expectation of that fulfillment.

We might begin with Zechariah as the immediate prelude to Christ's coming, for it was to this old priest that the angel promised a son, John the Baptist, who would prepare the way for the Messiah's coming.

Soon after his appearance to Zechariah, the angel Gabriel appeared to a young girl, Mary, in the small town of Nazareth. The angel told Mary, "Behold, you will conceive in your womb and bear a son, and you shall call his name Jesus. He will be great, and will be called the Son of the Most High and of his kingdom there will be no end."

Mary's response to the angel has echoed down the centuries as a fitting word for anyone called of God: "Behold, I am the handmaid of the Lord; be it to me according to your word."

Before leaving her, the angel informed Mary that her cousin, Elizabeth, the wife of Zechariah, was to have a child. "Mary arose and went with haste to a city of Judah, and she entered the house of Zechariah and greeted Elizabeth." To go from Nazareth to Judah in those days was a long and tedious, even perilous journey. Mary probably avoided two of the three possible routes, since one was used by Roman soldiers and the other was a long detour through the Jordan valley. She probably went through Samaria, even though "the Jews had no dealings with the Samaritans." In any event, when she arrived she greeted Eliza-

What began in Bethlehem has not yet ended—He will come again.

O LITTLE TOWN OF *Bethlehem*

BY ALVIN ROGNESS

beth with the news of the angelic visit in the beautiful words of the *Magnificat,* a hymn of praise so rhapsodic that it is still widely used in the prayers and liturgies of the church: "My soul magnifies the Lord, and my spirit rejoices in God my Savior."

When, three months later, Mary returned to Nazareth, Elizabeth gave birth to John. His father Zechariah, filled with the Holy Spirit, said of him: "And you, child, will be called the prophet of the Most High; for you will go before the Lord to prepare his ways."

Now to Bethlehem. Micah, the prophet, had foretold the importance of the town in the words: "But you, O Bethlehem Ephrathah, who are little to be among the clans of Judah, from you shall come forth for me one who is to be ruler in Israel, whose origin is from of old, from ancient days." There were other clues. Born in Bethlehem, the Messiah would be of the house and lineage of David, the great Israelitic king. He would be born of a virgin. He would be called out of Egypt; in the words of Hosea: "When Israel was a child, I loved him, and out of Egypt I called my son.

Perhaps no words in all Christendom have inspired such tenderness and even awe as this simple account by Luke:

> And Joseph also went up from Galilee, from the city of Nazareth, to Judea, to the city of David, which is called Bethlehem, because he was of the house and lineage of David, to be enrolled with Mary, his betrothed, who was with child. And while they were there, the time came for her to be delivered. And she gave birth to her firstborn son and wrapped him in swaddling cloths, and laid him in a manger, because there was no place for them in the inn.

The birth of this peasant child has given to the world its finest music and its most sublime art, and has released into the lives of people an unparalleled surge of joy and hope and love. Heaven came to earth, and the earth has never since been the same.

We who have sung Phillips Brooks' hymn, "O little town of Bethlehem," may find it diffi-

This door in the Church of the Nativity is the entry to the chapel built on the place where it is thought Jesus was born.

cult to substitute a stable and a manger for the Church of the Nativity, Built by Helena, the mother of Emperor Constantine, and dedicated in A.D. 327, the church was enclosed in the sixth century by a larger structure under Justinian. But the Judean hills are the same, and the same stars shine at night. With a little imagination, the enchanting story of the birth, angels, shepherds, the star, and the Wise Men can be reclaimed. Despite the jostling stream of pilgrim-visitors and the highly ornate interior of the basilica, to stand at the bare, stone entrance to the grotto is to journey back to the quiet night that changed the world.

The significance of the birth went unnoticed by most of the throng that came to Bethlehem for the census, but Joseph and Mary must have been overcome by the strange things that happened. How could they account for the shepherds who came to report that they had received the message from the angel: "Be not afraid; for behold, I bring you good news of a great joy which will come to all the people; for to you is born this day in the city of David a Savior, who is Christ the Lord. And this will be a sign for you: you will find a babe wrapped in swaddling cloths and lying in a manger." With what awe and wonder they must have reported further that a multitude of heavenly host had joined the angel, praising God and saying, "Glory to God in the highest, and on earth peace among men with whom he is pleased!"

Joseph and Mary followed to the letter the customs of Judaism; Jesus was circumcised on the eighth day and 33 days later was presented in the temple. There, again, a strange thing happened. A just and devout man named Simeon, seeing the baby, took him in his arms and broke out into these words of prophesy and prayer:

> Lord, now lettest thou thy servant
> depart in peace,
> according to thy word:
> for mine eyes have seen thy salvation
> which thou hast prepared
> in the presence of all peoples,
> a light for revelation to the Gentiles,
> and for glory to thy people Israel.

Persuaded by strange signs that a great king was to be born, Wise Men or Magi from the East, led by a star, came to adore and to bring gifts. Unfamiliar with the prophecies of Israel, they stopped in Jerusalem to ask King Herod about the newborn king. Herod's scribes, going back to the prophecies of Micah, directed them to Bethlehem, and the star led them to the stable. Warned in a dream not to let Herod know about the child whom he intended to kill as a possible rival to his throne, the Wise Men returned to the East by a different route.

Herod, enraged by being thwarted, ordered all baby boys under two years of age to be put to death. Meanwhile, warned of danger by an angel, Joseph and Mary had fled to Egypt with Jesus and did not return to their homeland until Herod had died. They then came to Nazareth, where Jesus spent his boyhood and early manhood.

Jesus was 30 years old when he began his public ministry. Not until after his resurrection, three years later, did the events of that first Bethlehem night take on meaning. So far as any records are concerned, the strange events surrounding his birth were quite lost, except of course in the cherished memories of Joseph and Mary, the few shepherds, and the Wise Men from the East. These few people must have lived during the intervening years with anticipation for what the future would hold for this Bethlehem child.

The early disciples of Jesus, those who followed him in Galilee, had a growing feeling that they were in the presence of someone truly great. But, even for them, it took the dramatic events of Good Friday and the first Easter to send them back into the Old Testament prophesies concerning the Messiah. What they found there was a striking confirmation of their hope that Jesus was indeed the Messiah. How could they mistake the remarkable parallels in Isaiah, for instance?

> He was despised and rejected by men; a man of sorrows, and acquainted with grief; and as one from whom men hide their faces he was despised, and we esteemed him not. Surely he has borne our griefs and carried our sorrows. . . . But he was wounded for our transgressions, he was bruised for our iniquities; upon him was the chastisement that made us whole, and with his stripes we are healed . . . and the Lord has laid on him the iniquity of us all.

And it must have been with great joy that they read this bracing description of Jesus, the Bethlehem child:

> For to us a child is born,
> to us a son is given;
> and the government will be upon his shoulder,
> and his name will be called
> "Wonderful Counselor, Mighty God, Everlasting Father, Prince of Peace."
> Of the increase of his government
> and of peace
> there will be no end,
> upon the throne of David,
> and over his kingdom,
> to establish it, and to uphold it
> with justice and with righteousness
> from this time forth and forevermore.

What began at Bethlehem is not yet ended. We have not yet come full circle. Born in Bethlehem, grown to manhood in Nazareth, suffered under Pontius Pilate, crucified, dead and buried, raised on the third day, ascended to heaven, seated at the right hand of the Father—the pieces of this divine jigsaw puzzle are almost all in place. One triumphant piece remains: "He will come again in glory to judge the living and the dead."

Those who have traveled to Bethlehem have been impressed by the beauty of the basilica, but they have also been drawn irresistibly to the simple stone entrance of the grotto. Standing there in silence or with hushed voice, one may forget for a moment all the "trappings," and can stand with the shepherds of old to see a baby!

The Church of the Nativity is located amid the busy throroughfares of the village of Bethlehem. Thousands of pilgrims come every year to worship at this place where once there was only a stable and a manger for the Child.

All followers of Christ understand intuitively that somewhere and at sometime during the bustle of the holiday, the purity of such a moment should be theirs. They may capture it in a church service, singing the familiar carols. It may steal upon them on a busy street as the refrain of some near-forgotten melody strikes the ear. It is altogether fitting that we be caught up in the merriment and joy of family reunions, of gifts and greetings exchanged. The Lord came to give joy. But to overlook the event of long ago that inspired it all is as a pilgrim lost in the markets of Jerusalem and Bethlehem, and never reaching the grotto at all.

Proveleon was not a wealthy village, but the people, God willing, were able to put something in the poor box.

THE CHRISTMAS *Caper*

R. D. STEVENS

T hen you cannot help us, Monsieur Demeron?"

"Cannot!" the baker snorted, his eyebrows drawn fiercely together beneath the ever-present dusting of flour. "WILL not, you mean! Go ahead and say it, Brother Joseph; I know you think it! Help you and your good-for-nothing poor? I'd be taking the bread from my own mouth to feed those brats if you had your way! A priest-ridden village if I ever saw one!" His voice took on the cringing whine of a professional beggar. "Alms, for the love of God, alms. . . . A few sous, your worship? A cabbage leaf, madame, a crust of bread."

Brother Joseph yanked the collar of his threadbare coat farther up around his ears and plunged from the warmth of the bakery out into the drizzle that was Proveleon. His thin, blue-veined hands trembled as he clutched at the crown of his hat, partly to keep the mistral from snatching it from his head, partly to hide the tears of vexation that stung his eyelids. No food for the poor, no food for the poor at Christmas, his sandals seemed to repeat as they clattered over the cobbles, and the faces of Mario and Lepanto

and Marguerite and all the others who'd held out their bowls for the last of the gruel that morning swam blurrily before him. And the donkey, thin sad beast that he was, had even stuck his head over the partition into the kitchen of the hovel and looked hopefully at him. Brother Joseph had given him the last remaining hay that morning— a few wisps and a corncob—and turned away quickly before the animal finished. There'd be no more tomorrow.

Brother Joseph stumbled as a gust of wind whipped the overly-large coat between his legs, and he went down on his knees with a jar that wrung a cry of pain from him. There was a clink, and the few coins he'd been clutching in one hand rolled soullessly down the steep street toward the bay far below. Brother Joseph lurched to his feet, ignoring the pain in his knees. "The coins!" he cried. "For the poor!"

Half a dozen urchins darted from nearby doorways; eager hands snatched up the coins as they rattled past, and the street was empty once more.

"Michel!" Brother Joseph ordered. "Alain! I know you. Come back here with those coins!" Again he called, a note of desperation in his voice now, and finally a woman's arms thrust two reluctant little boys out into the street to face Brother Joseph. He looked the sullen little boys up and down, eyed the ribs visible through holes in their shirts, the bare feet blue with the cold, and sighed. "Keep them, young ones," he said as gently as possible, and sent them scooting back to their doorway. "You need them more than I."

Once again the street was empty. Brother Joseph bent his head against the mistral and started for home. The hills of Proveleon were steep; the mistral strong; the sky a tattered gray that boded no good. He found himself wishing for his staff; the bruised knee wouldn't bother him quite so much with a staff on which to lean. He stumbled onward, past the square of yellow light thrown by the tavern windows, and paused for a moment by the door, set slightly ajar. The warmth,

the fragrance of wine and roasting beef were almost too much for him; he turned giddy and would have fallen if it hadn't been for a hard-muscled arm that slipped around his shoulders and held him firmly until the dizziness passed and he could stand once more.

"Merci, M'sieur," he stammered, aware of the flush creeping up his cheekbones. "A momentary weakness; it is of no importance."

He felt the sudden sharp scrutiny of his rescuer and blushed the more for the figure he knew he must appear, an old man in threadbare clothing. Clean, it is true, and patched, but with a definite odor of donkey clinging to it. The stranger—for no villager wore a gray corduroy jacket and trousers, or expensive if well-worn boots—the stranger must think him a beggar. Even his robe had long since gone for a few more francs to help fill the mouths of his brood.

"In that case, M'sieur," the stranger's quiet voice murmured, "you could have no objection to joining us for dinner."

Brother Joseph's head came up, his weak eyes peered at his rescuer. "I—I have—just eaten," he muttered and turned his head away to hide the longing aroused in him by the sight of a sideboard set with roasts and breads of many kinds and cider, HOT cider.

The stranger glanced at his companion, until now half-hidden in the shadows, and raised one eyebrow inquiringly. The old man heard a merry laugh, felt a smooth cool arm slip around his waist, a tiny hand pat his old gnarled one. "Then of course you will join us for at least a mug of cider, Brother. . . ."

Brother Joseph would not have been human if he hadn't reacted to the charm, the sympathy

in that voice. "Joseph," he managed, and raised his head to gaze at one of the most enchanting young creatures he'd ever met. Even the heavy seaman's sweater and beret could not hide the delicate triangle of a face, the huge dark eyes, the smoke and ivory that was Morgana, called "la fey." And of course Brother Joseph suffered himself to be led inside to a table and was seated across from the two young people, where the warmth of the fire could soak into his back, and somehow he found himself devouring a huge platter of roast beef while his host and hostess exchanged light banter. Brother and sister they were, on a cruise along the southern coast of France. Their sloop had been pinned in harbor by the mistral, and they didn't expect to sail until it abated. Actors, he thought he'd heard them say; at least they soon had him chuckling delightedly at their antics in one performance. It felt good to laugh again. It stretched long-unused muscles, and Brother Joseph found himself relaxing for the first time in months, basking in the warmth of the fire and the charm of his hosts.

"You are from Paris, then?" he asked, trying to place a faint *soupçon* that hinted of the North.

"Among many cities, M'sieur," the young man replied courteously and poured Brother Joseph another glass of cider.

"And you are actors?" Brother Joseph probed.

"Of a sort," the young man said and exchanged a secretly amused glance with his sister. "Of a sort."

Brother Joseph blushed. Perhaps it was the cider, or the warmth, but he was gabbling like an old gossip. "Forgive me," he said contritely. "I didn't mean to pry."

"You didn't." There was a hint of laughter in the young man's voice now, and Brother Joseph found himself studying him curiously. He was perhaps 28 or 29, with a thin, almost delicate face, dark eyes with a hint of jade to them, thin, well-cut lips. No one would ever call him handsome, but there was a certain lazy grace to his movements, a deftness with which he evaded Brother Joseph's questions that marked him as someone definitely—unusual.

It grew dark; the angelus was sounded, and Brother Joseph found to his dismay that he had talked for nearly two hours. Warm, relaxed, his stomach tight, and best of all, a kerchief full of beef slices to take home to his orphans, he found that he'd told his young hosts the whole story; it had spilled from him like poison spilling from a half-healed wound.

Proveleon was not a wealthy village, to be sure; the fishing had gone since the harbor silted up, and the thin, rocky soil did not produce much. But the people, God willing, were able to put a little something into the poor box now and then: a few sous, a few wizened apples, ducks' eggs, a cabbage or two. And the children helped. They were all orphans, many of Spanish or Algerian descent and, therefore, outcast. But the boys fished and hunted shellfish in the tide pools, while the girls hired out to clean and took turns herding the donkey up to the cliff pastures. Everyone shared alike, down to the last mussel divided between all twelve, or the last apple shared with the donkey. But the offerings grew fewer and the odd jobs harder to find, until at last the orphans were actually starving—the boys so weak their muscles trembled in spasms from the least exertion. Brother Joseph had watched with despair, spent every franc of his savings and his meager war veteran's pension on them, but still the day came when nothing was left. He'd gone out that morning, determined to find help, only to be told with the inevitable shake of the head that the saints must provide, mortal man had done all he could. Nowhere was he offered a scrap of work, a crust of bread, a suet pudding—although the smells of the butcher's shop had made his mouth water, and surely those were new shoes the greengrocer's wife was wearing? And wasn't the shoemaker's family looking fat and fit, and the grain in the miller's warehouse almost overflowing? But the baker was the worst. A devout atheist, he proclaimed himself, though when he'd had the pox he'd been quick enough to yell for the priest. A child hater too. Orphan he'd been, he bragged at the tavern; man and boy, he'd risen by the sweat of his own brow, and everyone else could too. The holy Sisters of Mercy, who'd secured him an apprenticeship as a baker, were conveniently forgotten. No sniveling was going to get so much as a petit pan from him. And when Brother Joseph, shivering with the cold, had pleaded with him, he'd been driven with curses out into the streets.

When the old man had gone, with many thanks and a lightness to his step that had been absent many a day, the two young people sat quietly, lost in thought. Remembering, perhaps, other orphans and times not so long past.

"Act One," said the young man thoughtfully, "to the baker." He frowned into his wineglass.

"Act Two," nodded Morgana. "The plot thickens."

"Act Three," the young man glanced up, smiling at Morgana's eagerness. "About to begin."

The mistral blew itself out two days later, but still the sloop belonging to the two young strangers tugged at her moorings in the harbor. They'd found the village pleasant, they replied courteously when asked, and the seafood good. Often they strolled the cobbled streets, pausing now and then to peer inquisitively into shop windows—the bakery, for example, where M. Demeron and his wife made those luscious rolls and breads and cakes that were displayed in the window. If they settled themselves on benches on the shady side of the inn and if their glances often strayed to the bakery directly across from them until they knew the ritual of M. Demeron's day as well as he, why, it was cool there, and shady, and the scent of roses pleasant.

The tiled roofs of Proveleon were already pink with the dawn when M. Ambroise, the policeman, turned into the main street. He had walked his small beat for twenty years without discovering more than a strayed goat in someone's garden. And he therefore amused himself by making his stride as regular, as mechanical as that of the sergeant of the gendarmerie, whose keppie, if nothing else, he admired. So it was this morning. Two strides, flash his light at the door of the butcher's shop, rattle the handle; another few strides, the grocer's shop.

M. Ambroise then did something he had never done before. He actually broke that well-practiced stride and came to an astonished halt. Village gossips would shake their heads over so momentous an event for years afterward. But quickly M. Ambroise's nose confirmed what his eyes had told him. M. Demeron the baker never, but never came to work before nine. At precisely that hour he would stalk down the street, produce a large key, and open the bakery. He had never varied the ritual in the twenty years M. Ambroise had been village policeman. Yet today, Christmas morning, the baker's shop was open, the red light of dawn reflected in its windows. M. Demeron himself in his white apron was sweeping off the steps, and his wife, that silent, long-suffering woman, was in the back of the shop taking bread from the ovens with the paddle.

"Good morning, M. Demeron," M. Ambroise called, not expecting an answer, and turned away, back to his beat. But then the second surprise of that memorable morning occurred. M. Demeron dropped his broom and ran toward the policeman, overwhelming him with a hug. "M. Ambroise, the very man! Come, try a croissant. They are fresh from the oven. And a roll, or a petit pan—perhaps you would prefer some cake!"

M. Ambroise found his arms filled with the fragrant morsels and could only stare, bewildered, at M. Demeron. "Are you feeling all right, M. Demeron?" he inquired solicitously. "Your liver has perhaps been troubling you?"

The baker laughed and clapped him on the shoulder. "The old woman and I are playing Pere Noel today, M. Ambroise, that is all. I am selling all my pastries at half price this morning, the

breads at two for a franc. Or even"—he shot a sly glance at his wife and lowered his voice — "five napoleons for a KISS! No, don't look at me like that, man, I'm not crazy! My wife and I, we planned this—a Christmas surprise for the whole village. Go on now, M. Ambroise, try them; they are very good," and he went back to his ovens.

Before M. Ambroise could begin on his eclairs, the fragrant smell of hot rolls had drifted out into the streets, and a stray child appeared, and then another. It was not unknown for these

street urchins to distract merchants long enough for another to snatch an apple or perhaps a loaf of bread or even a sausage, and dash off with it, handing it off to another if the angry pursuer got too close. But no sooner had they appeared this morning than M. Demeron himself appeared on the steps of the bakery, not waving his bread paddle at them as usual, but with his apron overflowing with rolls. Such a swarm of hungry, half-clothed little starvelings was never seen before or since! And by the time the sun was fairly up, the street was thronged with cheerful crowds, maidens laughing as they exchanged a kiss for five napoleons or a peck on the cheek for a croissant. Soon the baker's counters were bare, his money box heaped with francs, sous, a few lire, the beggars staggering homeward under great loads of bread. Brother Joseph and his crew of hungry orphans were munching on rolls; even the donkey had his few. Quiet came back to the street. One by one, the lights in the baker's shop were turned off, cupboard doors hastily shut, the coins scooped up into a canvas bag, and M. Demeron and his wife slipped wraith-like into the shadows that still lingered in the streets.

M. Demeron, the baker, took his great key from his pocket and unlocked the door of his shop. It was nine o'clock Christmas morning, and the slanting rays of the early sun were beginning to reach his windows. He padded across the floor, ignoring the light switch. Why waste electricity, was his philosophy, when in a little while the sun would provide light, and he knew his way blindfolded? A thrifty man, the baker. He felt the familiar roughness of his apron on the peg where it always hung, tied it around him, then turned sleepily to the flour bins. He pulled one open, reached inside. His fingers encountered only hard wood. He groped further, still half asleep, and found nothing. With a grunt he turned and padded across to the fireplace. A little light would soon put things to rights; he must have reached into the wrong cupboard.

The flames licked hungrily around the log he tossed in, sending shadows flickering across the ceiling. Surely that would dispel this nightmare born of sour wine and greasy bacon! He thrust his head into the bin and stared in disbelief. Empty! He patted the wood mechanically, but found only a trickle of flour in the far corner. With a queer feeling in his stomach, he crossed to the other cupboards and yanked them open. They, too, were empty.

He switched on the lights, ignoring the fact that the sun would soon be pouring its beams into the shop, and stood aghast. The shelves were all empty; the oven still glowing. There were fingerprints on his glass counter, trails of flour from the cupboards to the mixing tables.

The roar that followed brought M. Ambroise running from the tavern where he was relaxing over a late breakfast. A deliriously happy Brother Joseph, the mayor, and many of the townspeople followed.

"M. Demeron!" they shouted, surrounding him with sticky fingers and jelly-ringed mouths and enthusiastic embraces. "We love you!"

"Police!" M. Demeron managed to yell, freeing himself with difficulty from the grasp of two of Brother Joseph's orphans. That worthy stepped forward, his face beaming, "It was a wonderful thing you did, M. Demeron, the best Christmas the town has ever had. And to

think that, if it hadn't been for the two young strangers who saw you sneak up to the orphanage and leave the money, we would never have guessed!" A babble of sound, of congratulations drowned out the baker's incoherent replies, until he stood helplessly silent, his face turning beet red.

"Such a large amount of money, too!" put in one of the wives. "It should feed the orphans for many months. Even, perhaps, some schooling."

M. Demeron's face drained quickly of color, became its normal pasty white. Quite suddenly exhausted, he groped for a chair.

"But . . . but . . . I didn't . . ." he stammered.

"No false modesty is permitted, M. Demeron!" the mayor said, patting his shoulder kindly. "You shall have a medal at the least! A statue, if the funds can be found!"

"How did you do it?" chorused all the voices, and M. Demeron saw around him all the people of the village he'd known—and yet not known—for so many years. There was Mme. Reboult, her gouty leg not so funny any more, her face beaming with tears of joy; and the postman, retired for years, waving one of the baker's best soft rolls. M. Demeron felt his miser's heart contract at the sight. And the urchins nestled trustingly around his knees, getting sticky fingers on his expensively-polished shoes.

Somewhere inside him a hard, ugly scab broke loose.

He took a deep breath and tried hard to look sly. "It wasn't easy," he began. "We had to fool you all, my old woman and I. . . ."

"Ahhh?" they breathed.

M. Demeron settled down to talk, his gestures growing more expansive, his voice more confident as his tale unfolded. He laid a floury finger aside his nose. "It was this way, you see. . . ."

At the back of the crowd stood the two young strangers, almost invisible in the shadows of the greengrocer's shop. M. Ambroise might, if he hadn't been listening so avidly to M. Demeron's tale, have noticed a trace of makeup beneath the young man's jaw, the smudge of flour on his sister's elbow. But M. Ambroise had just finished his patrol, his stomach was tight with croissants and orange jelly and onion soup, and the warm sunlight was beating into his shoulders and gradually turning his bald spot pink.

The young man winked at his sister, and together they turned to leave.

The addition of a Danish Christmas plate to a collection is an eagerly anticipated tradition in thousands of homes around the world. There are two legends regarding the origin of the Christmas plate and plate collecting.

For the 1888 Scandinavian Exhibition of Industry, Agriculture and Art, the Royal Copenhagen Porcelain Factory produced an advertising plate displaying the company insignia or trademark. The plates, with a crown over three wavy lines (representing the three waterways through Denmark), attracted much attention. And when the royal family expressed an interest in purchasing them, a sign was placed over the plates for the duration of the exhibition: "Sold to Her Royal Highness Crown Princess Louise of Denmark." This plate is said to be the first commercial collector's plate.

In the second legend, at Christmastime wealthy landowners and merchants gave their servants and employees gifts of candy, cake, and food on plates made of wood or metal. Eventually the employers became aware that their employees were collecting these plates and using them to decorate their plain living quarters. The plates given by one employer were compared to those given by another. Consequently, the employers began to seek out more decorative plates on which to make their Christmas presentations.

Harald Bing, of Bing & Grøndahl Porcelain Manufactory, saw the potential in such a custom and in 1895 produced the first Christmas plate. This plate marked a significant step in the manufacturing and marketing of porcelain plates in that it was the first plate to be dated, leaving the customer with the clear understanding that there would be another plate next year.

More than one hundred years later these two Danish porcelain factories, under wraps of great secrecy, are still designing an annual Christmas plate.

Work on the designs for the Christmas plates begins two years in advance of the date the plate appears on store shelves. The designer for Royal

Under wraps of great secrecy, two Danish firms are still designing an annual Christmas plate.

CHRISTMAS PLATES: *Danish Blue*

LEONARD FLACHMAN

Copenhagen is given a general theme and on a specific schedule presents four or five art proposals to the design selection board.

Once the design has been chosen, a plaster model is made to show the relief affect on the plate.

Madonna and Child
Royal Copenhagen 1908

Star of Bethlehem
Bing & Grøndahl 1922

First It Was Sung by the Angels
to the Shepherds in the Field
Bing & Grøndahl 1911

Two years before a plate reaches the market, the artist begins work on the design. A committee selects one design from among several options.

Artist Kai Lange, who went to work for Royal Copenhagen at age 14, has designed 30 Christmas plates. His last design appeared on the 1985 Christmas plate. The work of a number of artists appears on the Bing & Grøndahl plates until 1963. The plate designs from 1963 to 1982 were done by Henry Thelander. Beginning with the 1986 Christmas plates, the work of two relatively new designers was introduced. The Bing & Grøndahl designer was Edvard Jensen whose work first appeared on the 1983 plate. And the Royal Copenhagen plate presents designer Sven Vestergaard.

Neither company has a master plan or list of themes from which the designers must work. There are, however, certain popular themes that reoccur on the plates of both firms. Danish churches and places of national significance are the most popular themes. Family situations occur most often on the Bing & Grøndahl plates, while biblical themes and Danish churches are common Royal Copenhagen themes. Both firms have issued a number of plates with biblical nativity themes. Birds, animals, and nautical themes are also favorites of the designers.

Contemporary themes were employed in the design of two Bing & Grøndahl plates. In 1940 the German army put King Christian X under house arrest in the Sorgenfri castle. That castle appears on the 1944 plate. At the end of World War II, an oak cross was erected in downtown Copenhagen to honor the young Danish seamen who lost their lives. That cross is memorialized on the 1946 plate.

Because the early plates are not available to collectors who have begun collecting in more recent years, Bing & Grøndahl has issued a larger, 9-inch plate every five years since 1915 that presents a modified reproduction of an earlier design. The designs of the following years have been reproduced on the 9-inch plates: 1895, 1900, 1901, 1907, 1909, 1910, 1914, 1915, 1926, 1928, 1936, 1941, 1947, and 1950.

Royal Copenhagen issued two Christmas plates in 1911. One plate, showing a snow-covered landscape with a lake, trees, and church, was rejected and withdrawn from the market. About 120 plates, however, were sold.

The first Christmas plate issued by Royal Copenhagen in 1908, "Madonna and Child," was also issued in a German, *Weihnachten* version. The 1909 plate was issued in two additional versions, French (Noel) and Czech (Vanoce). In 1910 an English (Christmas) version was added. In 1941 the English version was dropped, whereas 1943 was the last year for the Czech version. Following production of the 1944 Christmas plates, the French and German language versions were discontinued.

For centuries Europeans were enamored with the high glaze pottery that trading companies brought back from China. The pottery was called porcelain because its eggshell color resembled the cowrie shell of the sea creature known as *porcella*. Thus, it became known as *porcellana*.

It took several hundred years, however, for European chemists and pottery manufacturers to unlock the secret of the Chinese porcelain. Today the ingredients of clay (kaolin), feldspar, and quartz are ground into a fine powder, mixed with a green dye and water, and formed into large, semi-firm paste pillows to await the production of the plates.

The master modeler carves the artist's design into a plaster model, creating the bas-relief effect that typifies the Christmas plates. This model becomes the master for plaster of paris working molds.

The waiting green materials are mixed with water to produce a liquid porcelain, which is then poured into the plaster of paris molds. The plaster of paris quickly absorbs the water and a firm but fragile plate with a bas-relief design emerges. The green color of the porcelain enables those who remove the plates from the mold to determine if any of the white plaster of paris mold chipped off into the plate.

As soon as the plates have dried in the air, the green color disappears and the now cream-colored plates are moved by a slow-moving conveyor through a kiln. As a result of this 950 degree firing, a hard, but still fragile, bisque plate appears.

The plates are now ready for the application of the paint, which combines cobalt oxide and gold. This water-base blue color is sprayed over the surface of the plate. With a soft brush the artist removes the color in specific areas of the design. A second coat of the blue color is then sprayed on the bisque plate. With a shaped chamois "brush" the artist removes color from other specific areas of the design and the plate is sprayed lightly a third time. After firing, the blue

The Magi
Royal Copenhagen 1910

The Flight of the Holy Family to Egypt
Royal Copenhagen 1943

A master modeler creates a plaster bas-relief model of the selected plate design which becomes the model for plaster of paris working molds.

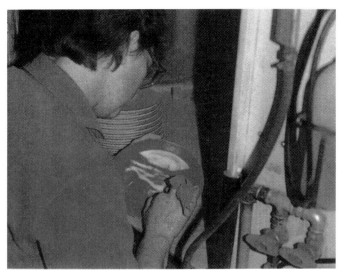

Using brushes and a soft cloth, the decorator carefully removes excess color to achieve the blue and white tones. The deeper the color coat, the darker the color will be.

Each Christmas plate is signed by the decorator before glazing.

Before the final firing, the plates are immersed in a quartz and feldspar liquid glaze, turning them milky white. In the firing the glaze melts, bonding the color to the plate.

color will be darkest where three layers of the blue color remain.

The blue plates, with very little of the design detail showing, are now ready for immersion into the glaze, a milky white quartz and feldspar liquid. The plates emerge looking much like the original cream-colored bisque plates.

While in the kiln for the second firing, the intense, 2500 degree heat causes the plate to shrink by a seventh of its size and to sag, so that the shape that emerges is not the same as what went into the kiln.

Following the 15-meter, 60-hour ride through the kiln, the plates are given two final touches. Any rough spots that appear on the bottom of the plate are ground off and the base is polished. Each plate is then inspected against a checklist of 30 possible imperfections. Such things as air bubbles in the glaze, a flaw in the mold, or an imperfection in the color will result in a plate being smashed.

Although the inspection is thorough, no two Christmas plates are identical. Because each plate is colored by hand the shades of blue cannot be standardized. Plates appear in shops and stores in dark, medium, and light blue. Many collectors search carefully so that the tone of their new acquisition will match the rest of their collection.

Neither Christmas plate manufacturer will divulge the number of plates they produce each year; however, both have a ceremony each fall in which the original model is destroyed. Never again will that plate be produced. Next year a new design awaits those who treasure the Christmas plates.

A fired plate sitting on a bisque plate shows how much the firing changes the size, as well as the character, of the porcelain. Each plate is then thoroughly inspected.

O HOLY CHILD

MELVA ROREM

O Child within a manger gently laid
I feel thy weight of love upon me still.
From the beginning, since the worlds were made,
Has come the promise that thou wouldst fulfill
All need. And need includes thy love of me.
With Mary let me watch above his sleep
While hosts of angels sing a melody.
I would be counted one with those who keep
A sacred tryst with thee on Christmas morn.
As hallelujahs ring, as hearts awake,
Let me rejoice to know that thou art born
And that my heart is richer for thy sake.
Thou art a glory that will never fade,
O Child within a manger gently laid.

Three northern Renaissance Nativity paintings point to the Light of the world.

DIVINE
Radiance

PHILLIP GUGEL

In the portion of his Gospel read at Christmas, John associates Jesus' birth with the bringing of light to humankind and to the world.

Master Francke, the Master of Flémalle, and Geertgen tot Sint Jans were three northern European painters active during the fifteenth century who left us Nativity scenes where the light of the Christ child plays a prominent part. They present us with three appealing and, at times, unusual versions of the birth.

These northern Renaissance nativity paintings interpret Christ's birth with imagination and sensitivity. Using very different images and treatments of light, each points us to Christ, the divine radiance, the Light of the world.

Nativity

from the Englandfahrer Alterpiece, 1424, Hamburger Kunsthalle, Hamburg, Germany

BY MASTER FRANCKE

In his depiction of the birth before a cave topped with a miniature landscape instead of the customary shed, Master Francke defers to an earlier tradition seen in Byzantine painting from Constantinople. This is the only known surviving panel painting to show this setting. The angel's message to the shepherds takes place on the right horizon. Its red sky, full of parallel rows of gold stars, alludes to Jesus' future Passion, a curious feature of this night scene.

The naked infant, who lies on the ground, and the omission of Joseph indicate Francke used the story of Jesus' birth by Saint Bridget, a medieval Swedish mystic, for these details of his version. According to Bridget, Joseph is absent to allow Mary to spend time adoring her son. In a technique similar to the speech balloons for comic strip characters, a banderole with the Latin words for "My Lord, my Son" unfurls itself by Mary's head. The smaller than life-sized figures of the angels surrounding her emphasize her importance. Spreading out her blue mantle, they form "an improvised sanctuary" around her (Snyder). This is really a scene of Mary's adoration rather than a nativity

Above, God's bust-length figure floats within his cloud as he blesses her adoration. The rays of light falling from his lips intersect those surrounding Jesus and Mary's heads, bathing all three in a warm luminescence and reminding us of this light's divine source.

Painted as part of an altarpiece commissioned by a merchants' guild in Hamburg, Germany, which traded with England, the Nativity's vivid contrasts of warm colors impart a naive and winsome mystery, while placing Jesus' birth in the context of his Passion.

The Nativity

(c. 1420-1425) The National Gallery, London

BY MASTER OF FLÉMALLE

The principal figures in this painting crowd themselves around the front and sides of a deteriorating weathered stable set obliquely from the left foreground. The dilapidated state of the stable signifies the old world before Jesus' birth. In the background stretches a complex, imaginary landscape depicted in painstaking detail, bathed in silvery-gray daylight. The landscape, as well as the angels in their billowing gowns and banderoles, reflects the influence of French painting of the time.

A number of legends about Jesus' birth also influenced what the Master of Flémalle included in his painting of the Nativity. For instance, in the right foreground he depicted the two midwives said to be present at the birth. The one facing us extends her right hand; it is now healed, after withering when she doubted Mary's virginity. One of the angels had told her to touch the Child, which restored her hand (Cuttler). The Master of Flémalle also depicted Mary garbed in white and kneeling, as Saint Bridget describes her.

The background's brown, green, and gray tonalities serves as a foil that sets off the bright colors and ornamentation of the principal figures' raiment. The shepherds, peering through the half-open door in awe, counter the elegantly garbed angels and midwives with their unsophisticated expressions and poses.

Two other details from Saint Bridget's account of the birth appear: the Child lies naked on the ground and Joseph shields a lighted candle in his left hand. Shielding the candle makes perfect sense: the light brought by the Christ child, symbolized as in Master Francke's picture by the golden rays coursing from his body, exceeds any natural light in this world. His radiance brings life itself. For Saint Bridget, it "totally annihilated the candle flame's material light" (Panofsky).

The sun rising above the left horizon further emphasizes the power of the infant's divine radiance. With an eye at its center emitting light rays, the celestial image symbolizes the Child and heralds the rising of a new age marked by his birth.

ngels serve as a visual entry point into this small panel painting by Geertgen, which has been described as "one of his most tender and poetic works" (Snyder). An aura of calm pervades the ruined stable's glowing interior. The reserved expressions and gestures of the simplified figures of Mary, Joseph, and the angels are lost in devotion over the holy Child. Shadows mute their forms, and the incandescence bathes the oval faces and expressive hands of Mary and the angels so that they seem spotlighted against the darkness.

This heavenly light, radiating from the Child's glowing body remains the stable interior's only illumination. By limiting the light to this source, Geertgen draws all of our attention to the infant as the source of divine and material radiance. Not only is the Child's radiance dominant in the stable, it outshines the angelic light overpowering the shepherds' bonfire, as the annunciation to the shepherds takes place as a subsidiary scene in the distance. Only the Child's luminescence remains important for Geertgen, who, like the Master of Flémalle, has depicted Mary and Joseph without a halo.

Night Nativity

(1480-85) Musee des Beaux-Arts, Dijon, France

BY GEERTGEN TOT SINT JANS

SOURCES CITED

Cuttler, Charles, *Northern Painting from Pucelle to Bruegel/Fourteenth, Fifteenth, and Sixteenth Centuries*, New York: Holt, Rinehart, and Winston, Inc., n.d., 75.

Panofsky, Erwin, *Early Netherlandish Painting, Its Origin and Character*, Cambridge (USA): Harvard University Press, Vol. 1, 1953, 126.

Snyder, James, *Northern Renaissance Art Painting Sculpture, the Graphic Arts from 1350-1575*, Englewood Cliffs (New Jersey): Prentice-Hall, Inc., and New York: Harry N. Abrams, Inc., 84-85.

The celebration of Christ's birth is for many also a celebration of ethnic roots.

CUSTOMS FOR THE *Family*

The true spirit of Christmas is always anchored in the centuries-old story of God's eternal gift of himself in Bethlehem's manger. For many of those centuries the most common Christmas custom was to spend this resplendent holiday with family. As the host and hostess focused on feeding their guests, the customs of many lands center on foods. A Christmas tree, decorations, and gifts helped contribute to the festive air of the family celebration. In many countries, the great drama of the season was highlighted with the Christmas Eve service. The carols learned in church were taken home and sung again in family groups.

For over 60 years Christmas has highlighted the customs of many ethnic groups. For several generations of Americans, the celebration of the birth of Christ was also a celebration of ethnic roots. Often the ethnic character of the American family commemoration bears little resemblance to present day celebrations in the homeland. But we like to remember . . .

Denmark

The Danish Christmas season begins weeks in advance with preparations for the Advent wreath. The key element is the candle—candles in wreaths, candles in windows of homes, candles in churches. The children are introduced to the spirit of Christmas by the Advent calendar on which they find small gifts. Everyday the children open a small present until Christmas when the most anticipated gift is received.

Everywhere are decorations or *pynt,* the Danish word for trimmings for the house and Christmas tree. A tree is brought home before Christmas Day. The adults decorate it with handmade ornaments in the shapes of angels, birds, apples, hearts, and *nisser* (Christmas elves) plus real candles, which are lighted when the children are permitted to see the tree for the first time. Danes use hearts as a central theme in all their Christmas decorations: on the Christmas tree, as table decorations, baked goods in the form of hearts.

On Christmas Eve Danes go to church services, usually at 4:00 P.M., to allow time for dinner and family celebrations afterward. Home-baked specialties include the *kiejner* and *julekage,* marzipan tarts and vanilla wreaths. Red cabbage is a must, as is the traditional roast goose, accompanied by *leverpostej,* a liver paste that tastes marvelous on Danish pumpernickel bread. A special treat, rice porridge with whipped cream and chopped almonds, is made with one whole almond hidden inside. The person who finds the almond claims a prize—a piece of marzipan fruit.

After supper, each person goes to the head of the house and thanks him or her for the meal. Then the living room doors are opened to reveal the elaborately decorated Christmas tree surrounded by gifts. Everyone joins hands and dances around the tree, singing each person's favorite Christmas carol.

Norway

Christmas in Norway is celebrated with a rich blend of pagan and Christian traditions. Coniferous trees are so plentiful that they grace not only the homes of Norwegians but also the public buildings and open markets of every city and town. One favorite food of Norwegians at Christmastime is fish, not necessarily *lute fisk* which has become a tradition among the Norwegians in America, but fine fish of one kind or another. *Lute fisk* is, if anything, scorned at home. A 19th century method for drying cod, *lute fisk* was thought

to be of mediocre quality. Nevertheless it became a nostalgic delicacy for Norwegian emigrants and their descendants in America. The *julegrisen* (Christmas pig) is another favorite, yielding all sorts of holiday dishes including the feet which are considered a delicacy when pickled in brine. Norwegians are unsurpassed for their fine baked goods in the Christmas season. According to tradition, a homemaker must bake at least seven varieties, preferably 14 or 21 or any multiple of seven.

Rice porridge is standard fare on the Christmas menu. Some families serve it on Christmas Eve with one almond hidden in the entire batch. The lucky person who finds the nut receives a special reward, often a marzipan pig decorated with a red ribbon. On coastal farms in Norway an elfin tenant helper, called *nissen,* is believed to reside in the barn year-round to keep an eye on everything and everybody. His only annual reward is a bowl of the traditional rice porridge on Christmas Eve. But the favor is not one-sided. If the *nissen* empties his bowl, that's a good omen for the farmer as well as for the elf. It means he has a home for the next twelve months. If the bowl is not found empty, it signals trouble for the farmer because the good elf has decided to move elsewhere.

Not only elves but domestic animals—cattle, horses, pigs—all get extra portions on Christmas Eve. Birds are remembered with bountiful sheaves of grain that are posted in the yard or attached to the roofs of buildings in the farmyard. Here, too, the occasion has a prophetic intention: If large numbers of birds come to enjoy the benefits, the next year will be a good one for the farmer.

At about 4:00 P.M. on Christmas Eve, church bells signal the closing of stores, offices, and places of business. Families gather for a Christmas Eve supper, which may be more or less sumptuous depending on plans for feasting on Christmas Day. On Christmas Eve children wait outside for the tree to be trimmed and lighted. Usually the Christmas tree is decorated with traditional ornaments, foods, and small Norwegian flags.

Following dinner the family gathers in the room with the tree. The *jule nissen,* a Christmas elf, has already brought the gifts and placed them under the tree. Adults and children join hands and circle the tree, singing the most beloved of Christmas carols—for example, *"Da tender moder alle lys og ingen krok er mork"* ("Then mother lights the Christmas tree and fills the room with light"). Gifts are passed out, and merriment continues until late at night.

Sweden

Sweden has absorbed the traditions and the folklore of the winter solstice into the Christmas season. In rural areas green branches are hung out to remind the farmers of spring. Bundles of oats are hung from rooftops, from poles, or from the decorative greenery. Originally the oats were intended for Odin's horse on his trips to Valhalla, but today the birds are the beneficiaries in the dark, snowy Swedish winter. The Christmas season begins on December 13. This is the feast of St. Lucia (her name in Latin means "light"), the feast of lights.

On the morning of December 13, one of the daughters in each family dresses as Santa Lucia in a white gown with a red sash. She wears a garland of green lingonberry leaves crowned with lighted candles. She sings the old Neapolitan hymn, *Santa Lucia,* and takes coffee and freshly baked saffron buns, called *Lusse Cats,* to her parents in their room. Any other girls in the family also dress in white and accompany Santa Lucia with lighted candles. Sons play a part in the family procession too, wearing tall, cone-shaped hats decorated with stars.

There are several legends about Lucia. According to one, she was a fourth-century Sicilian girl who was engaged to a pagan noble. She gave her dowry to the poor and, when her fiance accused her of being a Christian, she was sentenced to burn at the stake. But the flames did not harm her body, and Lucia died only after being stabbed through with a sword. Another legend places Lucia in the Middle Ages where she brought food and hope to the starving people of Sweden. Regardless of which legend people believe, Santa Lucia is a symbol of hope and light.

The good elf *jultombe* (Christmas gnome) brings good things for children. They reward his arrival by putting large helpings of Christmas cake out for him to eat. On the farms the *julklapp* is still a tradition. This ceremony calls for families to gather at the windows of their houses and throw out gifts. In the strict tradition these gifts were straw figures of animals, especially horses, or people. The practice was supposed to bring good luck to the home and its dwellers.

The Christmas tree is today central to the celebration of Christmas in Sweden. Imported from Sweden's neighbors is the tradition of children dressed in white who go from house to house singing carols in return for candy and slices of Christmas cake.

The Swedes begin their Christmas celebration on St. Lucia by eating lots of *lussekatter* (saffron cakes). This expands greatly on Christmas Day when the *julbord* (Christmas table) might include pickled elk meat, turkey, rice pudding, and a generous *allmant smorgasbord* (a buffet of varied hors d'oeuvres). Most tables will include varieties of dark bread and *knackebrod,* a hard biscuit flavored with dill or fennel seeds. Desserts often consist of cheeses, fruits, perhaps pudding or fresh-baked cakes.

Germany

In Germany lights, particularly candles, carry powerful symbolic meaning for all inhabitants.

Advent in Germany is celebrated with stern intent. Wreaths with four candles can be found in homes, in churches, and often in public places and offices. One candle is lighted the first week of Advent, two the second week, and so on, until four candles are burning the final week before Christmas. Most German homes also have an Advent calendar with windows that the children open with each passing day of anticipation.

Common in Germany is the figure of St. Nicholas who delivers presents to good children on December 6. He is not without his demonic side, for in most areas he is accompanied by his mentor, Ruprecht, who is dressed in black. While St. Nicholas usually appears in the form of a bishop carrying his crozier, Ruprecht sometimes is referred to as "Black Nicholas." His duty is to admonish children and, if necessary, administer a few swats to those who have misbehaved.

On December 13 the school children of the community join together in the evening for a *lichterzug,* a lantern procession through the town. Often the lanterns are made by school children in their crafts classes out of wooden or wire skeletons covered with stretched material, painted colorfully, and housing a lighted candle.

The Christmas tree, popularly ascribed to Martin Luther, is lighted in the German home only with candles, thus superimposing on the natural symbol of perpetual life one that connotes the supernatural.

On Christmas Eve, to the melody of *"Stille Nacht, Heilige Nacht,"* children gain their first glimpse of the lighted Christmas tree, which illuminates the many gifts beneath. These were brought by the *gabenbringer* (literally, gift bringer) whom everyone recognizes to be the Christ child. Sometimes attributed to the *Weihnachtsmann* (Christmas man) or an angel, the gifts are prepared and kept in a locked room. The children are not permitted to enter the room before Christmas Eve when the doors swing open and the scene erupts in all its lighted glory. Most family members gather around the tree holding hands while they sing several hymns or carols before *bescherung,* the distribution of gifts.

A three-day event in Germany, Christmas lasts from December 24 to 26. The first two days are essentially for the family, the third for visiting relatives. When they have finished their rounds, in many German homes families gather one last time around the Christmas tree. They sing a few songs and for the last time that season extinguish the candles burning on the tree. The Christmas season, the feast of lights during the dark days of winter, has officially ended.

England

In England the customs associated with Christmas are woven into the fabric of their lives, and the traditions of the season are anxiously anticipated by everyone.

The Yule log celebration is central to the season for many in England, for the open hearth is the very soul of their homes, and the Christmas fire brings each family the burning heart of the season. Dressed in their holiday attire the father and the oldest son triumphantly lead the way pulling the newly cut log. Mother and the other children follow, carrying garlands of fresh greens from the woods. Each member of the jolly group sits for a moment on the log, hums a bit of a lilting carol, and salutes the log with a kiss—an assurance of good luck until another Christmas comes. When the time comes for the log to be lighted with a brand of last year's log, everyone watches intently; the throat tightens, the heart quickens a bit, and a moment of tenderness falls as the new log takes torch and glows.

The church bells, some deep and resonant, some clear and plangent, announce the good news that Christmas has come. Taking their Bibles, all go off to services which include familiar carols, bringing the appropriate nostalgia of the season.

Christmas is roast goose and steamed pudding, pantomimes and Mummers' plays. In early Britain wandering bards and harpers found their way to castles where their songs of chivalry filled the air. Now, outside the door, the voices of the "waits" suddenly break forth making the chill air sweet with their carol singing. Lighted candles in the windows, telling the story of the Christ child who wanders the fields and woods at Christmas time, signal welcome. The candle is a symbol of both cheer and compassion. And any wayfarer, too, who seeks warmth and shelter on a winter's night is welcomed in the Christ child's name.

Italy

Italian Christmas celebrations start with a *novena,* nine days of prayers. On the first day of the *novena,* each family sets up a *praesepio* or manger scene in the home. Some *praesepios* are elaborately designed, with angels suspended overhead and an entire miniature village laid out surrounding the lowly inn. The tiny handcarved or cast nativity figures are often passed down through generations of family members.

The manger scene may also be set up on the bottom shelf of a pyramid-shaped display gaily decorated with pinecones, candles, and colorful paper. This is called a *ceppo* and may take the place of a Christmas tree. Every morning, the family begins the day by gathering around the manger scene for prayers.

Francis of Assisi created the first manger scene on a hillside outside of Greccio, Italy, in the thirteenth century. Francis wanted to bring alive the humility of Christ's birth for his ill-educated people. So he converted a cave on a hillside into a manger using a live ox and ass. Costumed villagers represented Mary and Joseph and the other members of the nativity story. This first manger scene so moved all who saw it that the custom rapidly spread and today the *praesepio* (or the creche, as also commonly called) plays a major role in the Christmas celebrations of most Christian cultures. It is still the focal point of an Italian Christmas.

Puerto Rico

Navidades, the Christmas/Epiphany season in Puerto Rico, is marked by caroling of all kinds.

The Mass of the Carols, *Misas de Aguinaldo,* begins festivities on December 16 at 5:30 A.M. Before dawn each day until Christmas, the devout attend church services. These services are marked by robust caroling. After mass, the celebrants carry the joy of the season with them by continuing to sing all the way to their homes and workplaces.

The music and carols do not stop with the Christmas Eve mass, called *Misa de Gallo,* but continue until January 6, the Epiphany. This is *the* big festival, and each town and village celebrates in its own traditional way. In Aguas Buenas, south of San Juan, celebrants gather before a painting of the Magi and sing carols. In San Juan, townspeople parade through the streets, which are gaily decorated with poinsettias and gold ribbons.

The highlight of the festivity is the *parrandas.* Neighbors go from house to house, playing guitars and serenading occupants. The hostess traditionally greets each visitor with a special song called a *copla,* which she improvises as each guest arrives. Visitors and householders end the visit with traditional carols and a toast for the season and friendship. The celebrants go off to the next house, where the singing, caroling, and toasting begin again. The *parrandas* continue until dawn, when the Christmas season comes to an end.

The story of the star of Bethlehem as seen by an astronomer.

THE STAR OF *Bethlehem*

KARLIS KAUFMANIS

The charming Christmas story as we find it recorded in the second chapter of Matthew is well known to all of us. Wise Men came from the east to Jerusalem saving, "Where is he that is born King of the Jews? For we have seen his star in the east and are come to worship him." When troubled Herod heard of the strangers, he called the Wise Men and inquired from them what time the star appeared. Then he told them, "Go and search for the Child, and when you have found him, come and tell me so that I may come and worship him also." When the Wise Men departed from the king, a miracle took place: the star they had seen in the east was in the sky again, and it went before them till it came and stood over where the Child was.

This brief statement is all we know about the Christmas star. It may come as a surprise to sonic readers, for it is generally believed that our knowledge about the star and the ancient event itself is much more profound. We cannot even be so sure that the Christ child was visited by *three* Wise Men, as pictures on Christmas cards and countless pieces of poetry try to convince us. The only source of information we have is the Gospel of Matthew, and it does not say a word about the number of the visitors.

But every time Christmas rolls around, people wonder about the nature of the star. What was it? A divine phenomenon? A regular astronomical show? Or just a creation of imagination to envelop the Christmas story in a legendary light?

Planets Versus Stars

If the Bethlehem star, indeed, was a divine phenomenon, then an astronomer, of course, has nothing to say. But Babylonian writings and mathematical computations inform us of an extremely rare event that took place in the night sky about the time Jesus was born. The unusual celestial display was so beautiful and awe-inspiring that it was noticed and described even by stargazers who were other than Jewish. From the striking resemblance between what happened in the sky and the message of Matthew, it is reasonable to believe that the story of the star was coincidental with the ancient celestial show. To understand it, however, a few simple astronomical and astrological ideas must be introduced.

We recall from our school days that stars are distant suns. They spend their long cosmic lives so far in space that tens, hundreds, and even millions of years elapse before their light reaches us. Because of the tremendous distances involved, stars appear like stationary, motionless points in the sky. This is why The Great Dipper, Orion, and other constellations look tonight exactly as they did a year or ten years ago. And, we have every reason to believe that they will remain that way for many centuries to come.

But, in addition to stars, the night sky is frequently decorated by nearby luminaries called planets. Being members of our own solar system, they revolve faithfully about the sun and thus excel themselves on the stationary background of the starlit sky.

Little Bits of Jewish Astrology

There is nothing mysterious about their looplike paths. The laws governing the planetary motions are known so well that the positions of planets can be determined centuries in advance. But this was not the case 2000 years ago. As the ancient stargazers watched the sky, their attention was naturally caught by the swiftly moving planets rather than the "stationary" stars. As a result, a group of pseudoscientists called astrologers came into existence who asserted that the positions and motions of luminaries reveal future happenings. Everything is written in the sky, they claimed; one just must know how to interpret the celestial language.

Although astrologers have no scientific basis for their claims, it must be admitted that astrology has at times exerted a profound influence on human minds. It seems possible that the story of the star of Bethlehem coincides with an old Jewish astrological belief. But to understand the argument, three facts must be kept in mind.

First, two planets, Jupiter and Saturn, had a particular importance in Jewish astrology. Jupiter was called the King's star, while Saturn was believed to be the star of the Messiah. Prophet Amos called it "the star of gods," and an Old Jewish saying asserted that God had created Saturn to shield Israel.

Second, the sun and most of the planets move in such a way that they never leave the zodiac, a narrow band that stretches across the sky. The ancient star-gazers divided it into twelve equal blocks or signs. The sun passes through all of them once a year, Jupiter does the same job in twelve years, while Saturn, moving at a leisurely pace, takes 30 years to complete the trip.

To modern astronomers, zodiac signs are just rectangular areas in the sky used to describe positions of the sun and planets. To Jewish astrologers, however, they symbolized twelve different countries. The most important among them was the Sign of the Fish, believed to represent Palestine. No wonder then that many ancient astrological writings refer to it as the house of the Hebrews.

As the swiftly moving sun glides through the zodiac signs, it overtakes Jupiter and Saturn once every 13 months or so. When this happens, the planet disappears in the glare of the sunlight. With the passing of time, however, the distance between the sun and the planet increases, and the day comes when the planet emerges in the eastern sky shortly before sunrise. Known as the heliacal rise, the first appearance of the planet in

the rays of the dawning day had a particular importance in Jewish astrology.

Taking all this into consideration, Jewish astrologers predicted that the Messiah's coming would be heralded by a simultaneous heliacal rise of Jupiter and Saturn at the House of the Hebrews. This astrological belief was highly supported by an old but erroneous legend which asserted that a similar phenomenon had announced the birth of Moses.

When one considers how passionately the oppressed Jews longed for their deliverer, one can well imagine that their astrologers had never before waited for the heliacal rise of Jupiter and Saturn in the House of the Hebrews with such an impatience as they did about the time when Jesus was born. And then—after more than 853 years—there came the long awaited conjunction again! For more than eight months both planets remained side by side and during this time they passed each other three times.

The planet Saturn

The Magnificent Celestial Show

The magnificent celestial display took place in 7 B.C. During the first part of that year, Jupiter and Saturn were hiding themselves in the glare of sunlight and nothing seemed to indicate the approach of the grand event. But then it came. On the morning of April 12, shortly before sunrise, both planets emerged in the rays of the glowing dawn and—what was equally important—they were in the House of the Hebrews! Already close to each other, they kept getting nearer and nearer. When on May 27 faster moving Jupiter passed Saturn, the distance between them started increasing and it appeared that the show had come to an end. But astrologers did not realize that another surprise was in store for them. In the middle of July, both planets stopped the motion of recession and once more closed the distance between them during late September and early October, shedding upon earth their double brilliance throughout the nights. The fifth of October was the peak of this very rare celestial show. Separated by a distance of less than two diameters of the moon, the two planets formed an unforgettable scene in the dark October skies of the Middle East. The distance between them increased then a little until mid-November, when the planets started moving toward each other for the third time to reach the closest position on December 1. From then on, a new and, this time, a final withdrawal took place. Before they disappeared in the rays of the sun, however, they were joined by Mars, thus giving this unusually long and impressive parade of planets a grand and spectacular conclusion. But Mars, according to Jewish astrology, was the greatest enemy of their nation. One can well imagine how disappointed Jewish astrologers must have been when, toward the end of the bright and promising display of the two friendly planets, the symbol of ill omen entered the scene.

Was Jesus Born 2000 Years Ago?

This is what happened in the sky in 7 B.C. To see the probable connection between this event and the star of Bethlehem, we have to keep in mind that Jesus was not born 2000 years ago. Our calendar is based on computations of Dionysius, a sixth century monk, who calculated that Christ was born 753 years after the accepted date of the foundation of Rome. He erred.

It is known from Scripture that Jesus was born during the reign of Herod. But historians tell us that Herod died at least four years before the beginning of the Christian era. This brings the date of Jesus' birth close to the time when the triple conjunction of Jupiter and Saturn took place.

How the Star Guided the Wise Men to Bethlehem

What we have discussed up to now are hard facts based on mathematical and historical evidence. However, to restore the ancient event as it might have happened in those olden days, a little bit of imagination can be used.

First of all, who were the Wise Men from the east? Three kings? Rich pilgrims searching for the newborn Messiah? There seems to be little doubt that the men were Jewish astrologers from Babylonia who had followed the planetary motions, watching for the signs that would confirm the birth of the Messiah foretold by the prophets. But they had to wait for a long time. It was not until April 12, 7 B.C., that the heliacal rise of Jupiter and Saturn took place in the House of the Hebrews. When the planets met for their first conjunction, on May 27, there could not be any further doubt: the long-awaited Messiah had been born in Palestine.

It was now their duty to go to Jerusalem to find the message of joy. Since, however, the month of May marked the beginning of the hottest season in Palestine, it is likely that the astrologers postponed their trip across the desert until the cooler months of fall. And when they had the second conjunction—on October 5, even more impressive than the first one!—it must have encouraged them to leave immediately for Jerusalem.

Having spent from five to six weeks on their journey, the Wise Men could have reached Jerusalem by the middle of November. Their inquiries for the newborn King of the Jews brought them eventually to Herod, who asked them about the time the star had appeared.

From Herod's conversation with his high priests and the astrologers, we gather that the star could not be seen by this time. That agrees with the astronomical data, for by mid-November the planets were far away from each other. But while the Wise Men tarried in Jerusalem, the planets moved once more together, and on December 1—for the third time that year!—came to a conjunction. After sunset, the stars of the Messiah and the King would be seen side-by-side south of Jerusalem in the direction of Bethlehem, which was only a few miles away.

If the astrologers really followed the star, in about two hours they could have reached a place where the road turned southwest. But by this time, both planets had also turned westward and gleamed magnificently over the roofs of Bethlehem. Thus, the astronomical calculations agree amazingly with the message of the Gospel: "And, lo, the star, which they saw in the east, went before them, till it came and stood over where the young Child was."

This is the story of the star of Bethlehem as seen by an astronomer. Millenniums separate us from the days when the Wise Men carried the message of joy across the desert of Mesopotamia. But the yearnings of humankind for a richer and more perfect life have not ceased since then. All people still long for peace, freedom, friendship, and love. Despite the waves of evil and hostility that cross our planet now and then, the message of Christmas has lost none of its significance during the march of centuries, and the Christmas star shines above us with the same unceasing light as it did more than 2000 years ago.

The planet Jupiter

An emphasis on awakening the best in one's character through aesthetic experience.

THE BOYS CHOIR OF *Harlem*

THOMAS GOULDE

As December's dusk settles into New York City, the lamps above Martin Luther King Boulevard flicker then wax with an electric whine, as if harried awake by the fitful honking of crosstown traffic. From below, the patter of hawkers rises and falls with the call of greetings, laughter, and the din of commerce in any of a dozen languages, dialects, and accents. Here, on Harlem's great merchant thoroughfare, along sidewalks lined with vendor tables and stores festooned with lights and tinsel, streams of shoppers cross and eddy in a market scene as universal as humankind. All move to the city's beat, quickened by annual deadlines, by the shortened days, and by the chill of imminent winter, yet made buoyant by anticipation. Christmas is coming.

On one corner, opposite a Salvation Army bell-ringer, a Muslim tends a table of tracts and a charcoal burner in which nuggets of frankincense melt into smoke. The ancient scent drifts through the crowds, adding to the cold night air a note of remembrance and mystery. In the distance a church bell tolls.

At such an hour, in such a season, at any of a dozen churches throughout Harlem, one might hear a choir at practice. But just three blocks north, on 127th Street between Malcolm X and Adam Clayton Powell Boulevards, a very special choir may be found in rehearsal. Here, round a corner where parked cars have been known to lose their wheels, where streetlights cast into deeper pools of shadow and litter collects complacently in gutters, where in any season not all the faces are happy or friendly, the Boys Choir of Harlem makes its home in an old public school.

The holidays are an at-home time for the Touring Choir—those 35 or so boys who annually present upwards of 90 concerts across North America, Europe, and Asia, on trips lasting two weeks or more. This is a time for them to be reunited with the larger fraternity of choristers, to perform locally, to be with family and friends. Returning with them is choir founder and director Walter J. Turnbull, the broad-chested Mississippian and classically trained tenor whose vision of creating an all-boy choir on the English model in the middle of Harlem, has led the choir in its 24-year odyssey from a small church chorus to an internationally recognized performing arts, education, and human service organization.

The choir celebrates Christmas with numerous performances in various locales by several different ensembles. The boy trebles perform in the Joffrey Ballet's production of *The Nutcracker* for another season. And for several years, the full, 60-member Performing Choir has presented major Christmas concert at New York locations like the World Financial Center's "Wintergarden." The Touring Choir is usually booked for several corporate parties and other engagements. And in what has become a tradition, both the Girls Choir and the Performing Choir carol at area churches and hospitals.

The choir's regular concert format features three or more selections from the classical or serious modern repertoire, plus a medley of traditional Black music and a medley of popular Black music.

The traditional portion of the program is a spiritual heritage medley of four or five pieces. The medley celebrates the expressive and formal continuities of Black music from African drum chants through slave-days work songs and spirituals to modern-day gospel.

A popular section is a jazz heritage medley, comprising six to eight works that trace the ragtime and boogie-woogie roots of jazz from Scott Joplin through Fats Waller and Eubie Blake to Duke Ellington. A typical program, offering from 20 to 25 pieces, is packed into a solid two-hour concert (minus a 15-minute intermission, and plus encores). The choir adapts the regular program throughout the year to meet the needs of specific circumstances (such as Christmas) by omitting one or more of the classical works and/ or singing shortened versions of the medleys, then calling upon the Performing Choir's considerable reserves to fill any gaps. Where memory can't provide, a quick study will do. These boys have, on very short notice, lofted a Hausa welcome to Nelson Mandela on his first state visit, unfurled a patriotic welcome home for Desert Storm troops, made quick lunch of a jingle for a fast-food commercial, and learned a little Russian to toast their comrades in the Leningrad Boys Choir.

It is quite a mix of music for a choir that takes as its model the English boychoir. But choirmas-ter Turnbull does not hold with orthodoxy in such matters: "I know that we are dismissed by some critics because we don't stick to the classic or to classical choral forms, but I regard the boy choir and Western choral traditions more dynamically. What *is* important to me, and to our choristers, in the English tradition is its emphasis on the development of the individual, on awakening the best in one's character through aesthetic experience and building that self-realization through education. That, in a nutshell, is what the Boys Choir is *all* about. Once you understand *why* we sing, the question of what we sing assumes its proper dimensions."

In other respects, however, repertoire is of central importance. As an American choir director Turnbull encourages innovation and a degree of independence from the old forms, and works to represent American music as co-equal with European music. In his opinion, much music that is regarded as distinctly American—jazz, spirituals, gospel, blues, soul, rock and roll—would not exist without the contributions of generations of

Black musicians. So naturally, the repertoire includes those sources. In the task of trying to motivate young boys, Turnbull attests that having them sing music with which they can identify proves productive. In his words, "No sensible choirmaster would thwart such a happy development!"

The Boys Choir of Harlem has done more than simply restore neglected Black classics and

On their way to school, three students from the Boys Choir of Harlem Academy stop to talk on a Harlem street. Students at the Academy receive career and personal counseling, tutoring, as well as musical and vocal training.

folk music to the concert stage. It also has commissioned and performed new works by such Black composers as Kenny Burrell, Adolphus Hailstork, Hale Smith, and George Walker, as well as new arrangements by choir alumni M. Roger Holland, Howard Roberts, and Linda Twine.

With at least two-thirds of its program devoted to the work of Black musicians, why does the choir continue to perform the European choral classics? It's a question that gives Turnbull not a moment's pause: "Oh, there are a number of people who would have us do just that. Some of our audiences, I know, are only being politely patient during the classical segment of our concerts. They don't feel that music yet and would prefer we got on to the music with which they are more familiar. But I am a classically trained musician and am committed to awakening that sensibility in our children and, hopefully, our audiences. These are great and moving works of art, which ought to be part of everyone's experience and, I think, are a requisite of any musician's sound in their ear who judge the choir according to the degree to which it can match that sound."

"We don't and we won't," Turnbull says. "We are not a traditional, all-treble boys choir employing adult male tenors, baritones, and basses. We are an all-boy boys choir in which older boys sing those parts. And we do not teach our boys to simulate the Caucasian voice; it would be artistically illegitimate and potentially damaging to their vocal and psychological development." Instead, the boys are trained to use their voices in a natural manner so that they develop confidence in their vocal abilities and experience genuine pleasure even in the youngest singers. Add to this exacting standards for precision, balance, clarity, and expression, and the result is a unique and marvelous offering to the world of classical music, one that is rapidly gaining recognition.

Although he has sought it for nearly a quarter century, Turnbull is quick to assert that he is as surprised as anyone at the success and growth of the Boys Choir of Harlem. Asked to account for that success, he is liable to respond simply, "We have been fortunate."

By one reading of choir history *need* has always impelled its development. Begun in 1968 as the Ephesus Church Choir by Turnbull (then a doctoral candidate at The Manhattan School of Music) and Ruth Nixon, the choir was to be a low-budget, after-school program for the boys of one small congregation. The need for such a program was acute, and the choir was an immediate success; 20 boys enrolled the first year.

That success initiated a second motive to growth—the need to raise more money. By its second year, the choir was already concertizing in area churches and schools when Ephesus Church burned to the ground.

A third motive appeared—the need for a home. The choir moved to the Marcus Garvey Community Center in central Harlem and, as its ties to the Ephesus congregation loosened, began to change into a choir based in the broader community

Here a fourth demand arose—the need for more comprehensive supportive services. In 1975, the choir was formally incorporated as the Boys Choir of Harlem. Four years later, while enjoying a stable residence at the Church of the Intercession in northwest Harlem, it undertook to meet the needs of young women in the community through the founding of the Girls Choir of Harlem. In 1986, the choir moved back to central Harlem into its present home in the

Oberia Dempsey Multi-Service Center in order to address the educational needs of male choristers. The Boys Choir of Harlem Academy, serving 150 boys in grades four through eight, began classes.

The current annual budget of two million dollars (raised from performance income, major corporate supporters, foundations, individual donors, and grants from public funds) goes to support an enrollment of 220 boys and 30 girls in its program, which encompasses the Touring Choir, the Girls Choir of Harlem, the larger Performing Choir, several boys training choirs, the academy, and a parents association. All children receive career and personal counseling (as needed), tutoring, as well as musical and vocal training. The choir has hopes of further expansion—of a girls program equal to that for boys; of an academy that will include the high school grades; of developing additional ensembles to give more children more opportunities to experience the rewards of performance.

Artistic success has been a part of the choir's history from its earliest days, but the prominence of that success has grown along with the choir's public stature. In 1979 the Boys Choir made its first European tour (Holland, France, and England), which was the subject of an Emmy Award winning documentary, *From Harlem to Harlem: The Story of a Choirboy.* The tour was a critical success, and the film sparked a great deal of public interest. The choir returned to Europe in 1982 (the second of five tours), began to tour extensively throughout North America in 1983, and in 1985 made its first tour to Asia (returning in 1989 and 1990).

Since 1986 the boy choir has taken part in four recordings plus the soundtracks of two major films, the Oscar-winning film, *Glory*, and Spike Lee's *Jungle Fever*. The choir also was extensively profiled in Bill

Moyer's recent documentary film *Amazing Grace* and has appeared on various television programs and commercials.

It is an impressive record of accomplishment, and the Boys Choir of Harlem is committed to maintaining the momentum of its success. Such success attracts the opportunities that have allowed the choir to offset cuts in public and private funding with performance income and also attracts interest in its core program of child development.

Once a year the Boys Choir holds auditions, which are open to all New York City schoolchildren regardless of race, although most of the more than 3000 boy and girl applicants are children of color. Of the hundreds of children who display an ability for reproducing pitch and rhythm, the choir chooses candidates who evidence the interest and commitment necessary for further development. The choir accepts dozens more than it can afford, knowing that even this select group will be reduced by attrition.

Those that do make it are eloquent in their appreciation of what they feel the choir has done for them. Jimmy Kimbrough, who has been in the choir six years and, like many choristers, had no sense of his own abilities before being selected, says, "I tell people that you don't have to

The Boys Choir of Harlem performs a pop number. The choir's repertoire ranges from classical to contemporary, gospel, and spirituals. Two-thirds of its program is devoted to the work of Black musicians.

have a gift to join; they give you the gift!" Jose Suazo, who entered the choir at the same age as Jimmy notes the poor prospects of other kids in his neighborhood and says, "Every day I thank God, because I believe I am a blessed child for being able to be in the choir. I can't imagine my life without it." As academy students, both spend the school day at the choir but, like many of their fellows, cheerfully stay after school for tutoring, practice, and volunteer help in the choir offices.

While all feel the pressure exerted by their neighborhood peers, they have taken the measure of much that happens "on the street" and decide to let it pass. Tyree Marcus, age twelve, relates, "I come home to my street and I hear, 'Oh, you finally back from that dumb choir, you so stupid to be singing and not even get paid.'"

Members of the choir rehearse daily to prepare for over 100 performances a year. Choir members receive musical training as well as dance lessons.

Jose answers for him, "We do get paid. We get a good education and, if we do well, maybe a scholarship for college." Tyree finishes his thought, "Those kids think being a big star and making a lot of money is so important, but *they* have never been on TV or out on tour."

Tracey Sydnor, who at eighteen is spending his ninth and last year with the choir, is looking forward to a career as a professional singer and composer. He feels the choir helped him understand his gifts and use his talent. "You know even if you love to sing you can't expect to just go out and become a star. You need training. The choir has given me nine years worth of training." That training has had more than just a musical dimension, as Tracey acknowledges. "The choir

does train you for real life. I think of the choir as a job. You have to show up, you have to do the work, and then you get the paycheck, which is getting to perform in public or getting chosen for a tour."

Although touring demands sacrifice and sustained concentration, it is the goal of every chorister-in-training. It may be the only means for them to visit the wider world beyond New York City and doubtless seems the way to gain the worldly poise the older boys possess.

It certainly can be broadening for young minds. Jose, who went to Japan at age nine, recalls feeling a stranger at first until the abiding friendliness of the Japanese made him feel special. He also remembers puzzling over the large, neat packages he saw on the road from the tour bus window After some investigation, he determined that they contained the tools and materials of the road crews, and he was moved by the fastidious care given to such humble labor.

Tracey who visited East Berlin at age thirteen remembers the intimidation of bus searches by heavily armed East German border guards and the awareness that he had not felt such fear before. And he recalls the warm welcome and tearful response of his East German audience and the dawning understanding that, to them, he represented freedom.

Tyree, who feels the choir gave him the freedom to dream of possibilities and to do whatever he puts his mind to doing, had that outlook confirmed when he traveled to Hong Kong and saw "all these people living on boats!"

Jimmy who finds every tour exciting and is still awed by the graciousness of the audiences, thinks "the audience is key to making me feel good singing, especially at Christmas when they all sing along." Jose and Tyree enthusiastically agree, as Tracey sums up, "The main thing about the choir and performing and Christmas is spreading peace and joy."

Such stories of personal insight and individual presence, when multiplied by 35, or 60, or 250, begin to give a sense of why the Boys Choir of Harlem is so special and important an institution. They also may explain why its concerts on three continents have moved both sophisticated reviewers and untutored listeners to tears of joyous affirmation.

CHRISTMAS Music

MASTERS IN THIS HALL

William Morris

French
arr. Robert J. Powell

1. Mas - ters in this hall, Hear ye news to - day
2. Shep - herds man - y an one Sat a - mong the sheep,
3. Shep - herds should of right Leap and dance and sing,
4. "How name ye this lord, Shep - herds?" then said I,

Brought from o - ver sea, And ev - er I you pray:
No man spake more word Than they had been a - sleep.
Thus to see ye sit Is a right strange thing:
"Ver - y God," they said, "Come from heav - en high".

No-el! No-el! No - el! No-el sing we clear! Holp-en are all folk on earth, Born is God's Son so dear: No-el! No-el! No - el! No-el sing we loud! God to-day hath poor folk raised And cast a-down the proud.

5. Therein did we see
A sweet and goodly may
And a fair old man,
Upon the straw she lay:

6. Ox and ass him know,
Kneeling on their knee,
Wondrous joy had I
This little babe to see:

IN THE BLEAK MIDWINTER

Christina Rossetti

Gustav Holst
arr. John Seagard

1. In the bleak mid-win-ter Frost-y wind made
2. Our God, heav'n can-not hold him Nor earth sus-
3. E-nough for him, whom che-ru-bim Wor-ship night and

moan, Earth stood hard as i-ron, Wa-ter like a
tain; Heav'n and earth shall flee a-way When he comes to
day, A breast-ful of milk And a man-ger-ful of

stone; Snow had fal-len, snow on snow, Snow on snow,
reign: In the bleak mid-win-ter A sta-ble-place suf-ficed The
hay; E-nough for him, whom an-gels Fall down be-fore, The

In the bleak mid-win-ter, Long a-go.
Lord God Al-might-y Je-sus Christ.
ox and ass and ca-mel Which a-dove.

4. Angels and archangels
May have gathered there,
Cherubim and seraphim
Thronged the air:
But only his mother
In her maiden bliss
Worshiped the beloved
With a kiss.

5. What can I give him,
Poor as I am?
If I were a shepherd
I would bring a lamb;
If I were a wise man
I would do my part;
Yet what I can I give him—
Give my heart.

THE FRIENDLY BEASTS

Robert Davis, alt.

Medieval French
arr. Melvin Rotermund

1. Je - sus our broth - er, strong and good, Was
2. "I," said the don - key, shag - gy and brown,
3. "I," said the cow, all white and red,
4. "I," said the sheep, with curl - y horn,

hum - bly born in a sta - ble rude, And the
car - ried his moth - er up hill and down, I
gave him my man - ger for his bed, I
gave him my wool for his blan - ket warm, He

friend - ly beasts a - round him stood,
car - ried her safe - ly to Beth - le - hem town;
gave him my hay to pil - low his head;
wore my coat on Christ - mas morn;

Je - sus our broth - er, strong and good.
I," said the don - key, shag - gy and brown.
I," said the cow, all white and red.
I," said the sheep, with curl - y horn.

5. "I," said the dove, from the rafters high,
"I cooed him to sleep that he should not cry,
We cooed him to sleep, my mate and I;
I," said the dove, from the rafters high.

6. Thus ev'ry beast, by some good spell,
In the stable dark was glad to tell
Of the gift he gave Emmanuel;
The gift he gave Emmanuel.

WITH MERRY HEART

Piae Cantiones, 1582
tr. Maurice F. Bell

Piae Cantiones, 1582
arr. Paul Lohman

1. With mer — ry heart let de —
2. An an — gel's voice let all
3. The shep — herds sped to

all re — joice in one ; The Glo —
clared the Sav — ior's birth, ry to
see this won — drous thing And

moth — er maid hath now brought forth her
ry to God, good — will and peace on
found the babe, the which is Christ our

son In Beth — le — hem.
earth: In Beth — le — hem.
King: In Beth — le — hem. hem.

4. Both ox and ass, adoring in the byre,
In mute acclaim pay homage to our Sire:
In Bethlehem.

5. Now bless we Christ, eternal glory's King,
And Christ bless us, as to his praise we sing:
In Bethlehem.

Text from *The Oxford Book of Carols*, by permission of Oxford University Press.
Setting copyright 1983 Augsburg Publishing House.

WHENCE ART THOU

Traditional French Canadian
tr. William McLennan

Traditional French Canadian
arr. Normand Lockwood

1. "Whence art thou, my maid-en, whence art thou?"
2. "What saw'st thou, my maid-en, what saw'st thou?"
3. "Noth-ing more, my maid-en, noth-ing more?"

"I come from the sta-ble where, this ver-y night,
"There with-in a man-ger, a lit-tle child I saw,
"There I saw the moth-er her sweet ba-by hold,

I, a shep-herd maid-en, saw a won-drous sight."
Ly-ing, soft-ly sleep-ing, on a bed of straw."
And the fa-ther, Jo-seph, trem-bling with the cold."

4. "Nothing more, my maiden, nothing more?
Nothing more, my maiden, nothing more?"
"I saw ass and oxen, kneeling meek and mild,
With their gentle breathing warm the holy child."

5. "Nothing more, my maiden, nothing more?
Nothing more, my maiden, nothing more?"
"There were three bright angels come down from the sky,
Singing forth sweet praises to our God on high."

*The Hummel figurines—
a humble, innocent message
for Christmas.*

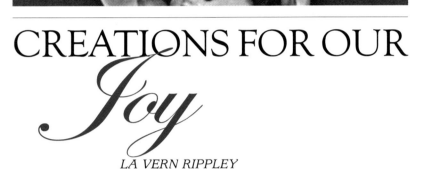

CREATIONS FOR OUR *Joy*

LA VERN RIPPLEY

From simple beginnings and humble surroundings, the Hummel figurines depict everyday events with a childlike innocence that has captivated the world's millions. With many parallels to the Babe in Bethlehem, Berta Hummel began her life in the tranquility of a remote Bavarian village in her native Germany and, throughout her life, retained the same unassailable spirit as the humble Carpenter. Even her religious name, Sister Maria Innocentia which Berta Hummel assumed as a nun, betokens the basic Christmas message. Her figurines, it has been said, provide everyone something to look back upon:

> Childhood is one main feeling that radiates. Innocence is another. The romance of youthful nostalgia is everywhere about them [the figurines], for that was Berta Hummel's style (a classmate, Otto Hufnagel).

Berta was born on May 21, 1909, in Massing, a town some 30 miles east of Munich and 20 miles north of Oberammergau, the passion play town. She was the third daughter of Adolf and Viktoria Hummel, and lived in the home where four generations of Hummels had operated a clothing store. At one end of Massing is the parish church of St. Stephen, named after the martyr whose feast day is celebrated during the Christmas season. At the opposite end of town stands the castle—convent of the Poor School Sisters. Originally a castle belonging to the counts of Massing, the convent's medieval, moated structure on one side and the Catholic church on the other dominate the skyscape of the village like bookends holding the inhabitants in the grasp of traditional piety. For centuries this village had functioned as a trade center, acquiring the name *Markt Massing*. This scene has been immortalized by the Hummel sketch, *Der Viehmarkt*.

Berta Hummel's childhood was simple but not immune from the turmoil of the outside world. Inspired and entertained by German folktales, the young Berta soon started writing plays based on these *Marchen* and performed them for her ever-widening circle of friends. Then, when World War I broke out, her father was drafted. Always interested in letters about suffering on the front, young Berta at the age of eight sent to her father colorful postcards which she had created to cheer and encourage him and his comrades.

She attended elementary school at the Massing *Volksschule* during the war. The Poor School Sisters were not always successful in disciplining Berta; she often sketched and drew pictures instead of paying attention, and her mother was called in for conferences on the problem. In the end, the tolerant Sister Theresa always promoted her, and after four years in the elementary school, young Berta entered the *Institut der Englischen Fraulein* (English Sisters' School) at Simbach, some 20 miles east of Massing. Here she benefitted from an art department and gradually caught up with her classmates in other subjects. At Simbach she learned watercolors, painted landscapes, and designed scenery and costumes for school plays. She also began creating pen and ink illustrations of the famous German fairy-tale characters she had learned to know at home in Massing. What Sister Theresa did for Berta at Massing, Sister Stephania did at Simbach. As an art instructor she could guide Berta's artistic instincts.

Sister Stephania suggested to Adolf and Viktoria Hummel that their daughter someday continue her art education at the Academy of Applied Arts in Munich. In spite of the troubled economy complicated by revolutions in Bavaria, a short-lived Communist regime, and years of disastrous inflation, Adolf Hummel accompanied Berta to Munich in 1927, where she enrolled in the *Akademie fur Angewandte Kunst.* The academy in the 1920s was one of the world's great centers of innovative art and design. Several directors of the academy were members of the *Deutsche Werkbund,* a professional association of teachers, artists, designers, and architects.

The *Werkbund* had its roots in south Germany, where Catholic tradition incorporated the baroque and Florentine outlook in its art style. South German piety called for more concrete symbols. The Christmas creche, for example, like the use of statuary in general, is distinctly a south Ger-

man phenomenon. Clearly, the young artist was influenced by this southern piety that was friendly to the Christmas creche. Her figures are fleshy, vivacious, and merry; they portray a creche-related childlike innocence.

While at the Munich academy, Berta studied with Professor Max Dasio who was famous for his illustrations in children's books and for his woodcuts of German folklore characters. He encouraged her to make frequent visits to the *Alte Pinakothek,* the famous classical art museum in Munich—a five-minute walk from the academy. In Munich Berta boarded at the Holy Family residence which was run with the strictness of a convent by the sisters. Always the court jester in this strict religious dormitory, Berta, in a typical prank, alleged one winter that she would invite male company for a *Fasching* party to be held in

the dormitory. The mother superior was relieved when the "visitors" turned out to be papier-mache models of her art professors, Max Dasio, Richard Klein, and Else Brauneis. Berta developed a close friendship with two of the Franciscan sisters and eventually indicated that she would join their convent.

During the following two years, Berta rose to the top of her class in the *Akademie fur Angewandte Kunst*. When she graduated on March 15, 1931, Dasio and her other professors asked her to stay on at the academy as a teaching assistant. The entire Hummel family traveled to Munich for the graduation ceremonies. Mindful of Berta's problems with discipline during her elementary school days in Massing, Adolf Hummel was at least outwardly quite surprised when his daughter announced that she was joining the religious life. After graduation, Berta journeyed to the Swabian town of Siessen where she entered the convent.

After her time as a postulant had been fulfilled, Berta received the habit of the Order of St. Francis on August 22, 1933, when the bishop symbolically cut away a lock of her hair and bestowed on her the name of Sister Maria Innocentia.

While Maria Innocentia was "sealed away" in the convent her message, broadcast through the medium of art, ignited the enthusiasm of the world. Already as a postulant she exercised world-encompassing influence by designing religious vestments and banners. All of them, in particular the chasubles worn during mass, bear the distinctive mark of her later Hummel figurines.

Many of her concepts were transported by missionaries as far as Africa and Brazil.

When Sister Innocentia entered the convent, it functioned as a teachers' college. Primarily, she taught art in the teachers' school, but she also traveled to some of the 65 schools administered by the Siessen convent to work with art programs for children. In order to teach and entertain young children better, she created a series of sketches which, in late 1933, were displayed for kindergarten teachers at a symposium in Rottenberg am Neckar. The productions were so well received that by mid-1934 several art publishers were vying for the privilege of publishing her works. Postcards with her artwork began to appear throughout Germany. Next, Maria Innocentia collaborated with Margareta Seeman in producing a children's book, entitled *The Hummel Book,* which greatly amplified the nun's popularity. Soon admirers and curiosity seekers thronged to interview her. Usually they were politely turned away, but on occasion Maria Innocentia greeted and visited with her fans, although not always revealing her identity.

Many legendary stories relate how Sister Innocentia's work gained public attention. One encounter with her artwork, however, proved to be endurable. In the summer of 1934, Franz Goebel, head of the *W. Goebel Porzellanfabrik,* viewed her sketches. It was "love at first sight," and truly there was born a savior for the family-owned firm with its 350 workers in the small town of Oelsau. Franz Goebel had lived for a time in the United States and Canada, and he understood the American hankering for ceramic figurines. In late 1934, therefore, Goebel traveled to Siessen to explain his export ideas to the religious authorities. Although reluctant at first, both Sister Innocentia and the convent director granted W. Goebel the rights to manufacture the sketches and drawings into ceramic figurines. The convent reserved and still retains final approval of all the three-dimensional designs based on her artwork.

Following visits by Sister Innocentia to the factory in Oelsau and by factory personnel to Siessen to present final models for approval, the first figurines, incised with the "M.I. Hummel" signature, were displayed for export at the famous world trade fair at Leipzig in 1935. The trademark officially protects figurines which were made from artwork created by Sister Maria

Innocentia Hummel after she entered the Siessen convent and manufactured by Goebel under an exclusive worldwide licensing agreement.

The same year, Sister Innocentia returned to the Munich academy where she began graduate study of the masters. At the same time she worked in the studio with chalk, charcoal, oil, and other experimental combinations.

As soon as "M.I. Hummel" figurines arrived in the United States in 1935, they were a raging success. A year later in 1936 the demand in the American marketplace expanded so greatly that big department stores like the Marshall Fields Company of Chicago became major outlets for the figurines.

Consulting with the Goebel factory to supervise new productions and studying in Munich soon upset Sister Innocentia's already fragile health. Stricken with influenza, she returned to the Siessen motherhouse to recuperate.

On February 6, 1937, the Nazi government decreed that all Catholic schools be closed and that taxes on convents be systematically raised to force them out of existence. During this difficult time, royalties from the Goebel factory helped the convent at Siessen to survive. Nevertheless, late in 1940, the convent was expropriated by local Nazi officials to be used as a repatriation center for *Volksdeutsche,* ethnic Germans who had been living for centuries in Russia, Romania, Yugoslavia, and other parts of Eastern Europe. Since the majority of these emigrants had come originally from Swabia, it was decreed that Swabia would be the center for "Germans from abroad."

At first Sister Innocentia went home to Massing, but in three weeks she was allowed to return to the convent to assist in the care of the 2000 returning migrants in the convent quarters. Living in a damp basement weakened her health. Further complications arose when Nazi leaders seized the convent's farmland and accused the nuns of conspiring to use food in excess of the war plan allowance, although they knew full well that the Franciscan tradition called upon the sisters to distribute whatever food they could give to the poor.

Frail and undernourished, Sister Maria Innocentia was x-rayed and diagnosed as having pleurisy and, later, a lung infection. In the fall of 1944, during the exhaustive German war effort, Sister Innocentia suffered a relapse and was sent to the Wilhelmstift, a hospital at Isny in the Swabian Alps. Here the earlier x-rays were reinterpreted to show that she was suffering from chronic tuberculosis. She recovered sufficiently to return to the motherhouse in time to see French troops take over the convent at Siessen on April 22, 1945, but by November of the same year she suffered a relapse and was removed to the Franciscan sanitorium near the town of Wangen. Complicated by dropsy, her condition worsened until the following September when she asked to return to the motherhouse, aware that she would soon die. At noon on November 6, 1946, Sister Maria Innocentia Hummel died.

In her eulogy the mother superior said, "The Master called his bride in the bloom of youth to the eternal nuptials. In a short span she has completed a long life." The world mourned her departure. The *Regensburger Bistumsblatt* said, "She, who has left this earth so prematurely, will continue to endow us in the future by her creations which she has left for our joy and edification, and which will continue to grow in popularity. From her early death, which she . . . welcomed with a happy smile that one finds in her childlike pictures, there goes forth a greater force than that which emanates from her precious creations—a force that sends comfort and strength into a time filled with sorrow and sacrifice."

Sister Maria Innocentia Hummel was a true disciple of St. Francis, the man of Assisi who is credited with having created the first Christmas creche. Throughout her art runs a Franciscan love of nature—birds, flowers, trees, and all of God's simple creatures. She never attempted to portray either social or spiritual problems, nor was there ever a hint of moralism. She simply exhibited what joy and humor were available in what was otherwise a drab, miserable world. She was, above all, an artist of children. She painted little people and old folks at their best by always placing them in charming settings that compel a smile. Her characters are often caught in amusing situations; they are happy mortals, roguish perhaps, but always innocent, like the name of their creating artist.

The Third Reich collapsed in 1945. Luckily, the town of Oeslau fell just west of the East German border when hostilities ended. Although politically free, the Goebel firm was nevertheless cut off from its prewar lines of supply and commerce. Aware of the Goebel predicament, the U.S. military government promoted commercial activity in the border region of West Germany and, along with other actions, lifted the wartime embargo of "M.I. Hummel" figurines. Many of the immediate postwar collectors proved to be American GIs stationed in Germany.

When the Federal Republic of Germany was reconstituted in 1948-1949, Goebel was already employing 800 workers. Advantageous exchange rates soon brought in American tourists who purchased figurines, as did military personnel.

New figurines have been authorized by the convent at Siessen. Six new designs made their debut at the New York World's Fair in 1964 and 1965. Seven other creations were released to celebrate the 100th anniversary of Goebel in 1971, which now employs more than 1500 workers. The same year, W. Goebel introduced its annual Hummel plate series. The company still has many new "M.I. Hummel" designs for figurines that will be released in due time; how many and when is a carefully guarded secret.

Since the production of the first three-dimensional ceramic Hummel figurine in 1935, about 450 different designs have been produced. Ceramic materials used include kaolin from England, feldspar from Norway, clay from Germany, and quartz from both Germany and Norway. After blending, the elements are magnetized to insure that no iron particles find their way into the figurines. After a complex procedure involving the making of several different molds, the working model is ready for casting. The slip is poured and left to harden for about 20 minutes, forming a shell. Cast in parts, the pieces are then sent to the assembling department, where they are reassembled and refined before the registered trademark is applied. Next they are fired, then dipped or sprayed with glazing compound, then fired again. Finally teams of artists paint the figurines, using over 2000 variations of ceramic paints. The figurines are fired a third time to bake in the colors. Many quality-control checks accompany these procedures.

In 1939, Sister Maria Innocentia visited the sanitorium at Krumbad and subsequently sent a gift to the sanitorium for Christmas. Marga Neises Thome later described her reactions on seeing this "M.I. Hummel" created Infant of Krumbad:

> Christmas 1939—a Christmas never to be forgotten, a Christmas spent, not with Berta Hummel personally but beside the crib whose Infant has been modeled by that famous artist. Evacuated from a city of western Germany. exiled and homeless, we found refuge at Krumbad, in the Convent of the Bavarian Sisters of St. Joseph. The sister superior told me, on Christmas Eve, that the Christchild which we were about to behold in the chapel crib had been made by Berta Hummel. . . . How marvelously Sister Innocentia had succeeded in expressing her profound admiration for the heavenly Child and what she had wanted to say: "Behold the extent of his love." A wonderful consolation, peace, and joy emanated from this poor Child in the crib. Here our restless longing for home was satisfied; here our lamentations ceased; sorrow was turned into resignation, yes even into joy. Here was true rest; I felt at home. Never before had the *"Et incarnatus est"* become such a living reality for me as in this hour, before this crib.

Like the Christmas story itself, Maria Innocentia Hummel's art needs little profundity or keen reasoning power to be appreciated. Even as the Babe of Bethlehem evaded the mighty Herod and his successors, so too, her art has overpowered and outlasted the scourge of Hitler and other worldly domination, simply sowing joy in the hearts of people everywhere.

ONE CHRISTMAS JOURNEY

IN Air Terminals, the country over,
loudspeakers are announcing flights
into the beautiful Blue Yonder, and holiday
travelers are taking off toward a "Whole New World"
of exciting sights, sounds and scenes,
"JUST HOURS AWAY,"
as the travel folders say!

(even unto Bethlehem)

Having fine time, wish you were here!

But for many of our Senior Citizens,
Christmas is a Season
of just A-SITTIN' and A-ROCKIN'
and REMINISCIN'

Some play "horsey"

Some just Snooze

Mother-in-law jokes cease when she becomes gran'ma "the sitter"

A Picture Story by Lee Mero

For THEM, we have arranged,
(and just MINUTES away)
"A TOUR of REMINISCENCE"!

All Aboard?

The Editor and the Artist.

GOING BACK TO GRAN'PA'S FOR CHRISTMAS meant, for city children, an exciting excursion through the snow-covered countryside!

RAILROAD CROSSING — LOOK OUT FOR THE CARS

EXCITING, because it was a brand new adventure! There was the jolly CONDUCTOR who punched the tickets, told jokes and tucked a slip in the band of father's derby. (He told US where to get off)

the NEWS VENDOR had magazines for those who liked reading and riding.

Mamma's favorite — The Ladies' Home Journal

VOGUE "the glass of fashion"

And in Collier's THE NATIONAL WEEKLY — where Papa got his jokes

Were those "Gibson Girls"

The "CANDY BUTCHER" had just about everything for those who chose to chew.

Candy, peanuts, crackerjack.

He became the HOT COFFEE MAN when lunch time came around

There was an unforgettable meal in the "Dining Palace on Wheels" (complete with FINGER BOWLS!)

FREE ICE-WATER

My, how you've grown!

And, finally the arrival midst piles of MERR-R-RY CHRISTMAS!!

THINGS WERE LIVELIER THAN USUAL on Main Street as holiday shoppers checked those "Last Minute Items" off their lists.

The "Lillian Russell" Hat (One "gift" a girl got—just for herself!)

the "STATUS SYMBOL" of that Era

Nothing like a gold watch and chain to dress up the front of a man! Except perhaps, a scarf pin, set with his stone, a loved one's lock of hair inside

A gold-headed walking stick for the pastor (from the Sunshine Circle)

A present for the Settin' Room

nothing like Arbuckles.

With the Coffee Pot ON and the Welcome Mat OUT folks were sure to drop IN!

Birth

Steckenpferd

baggage, bundles, boxes and milk cans on the depot platform, with "Hellos" and "Glad-to-See-Yous" all around from happy relatives!

look at the huggin' and kissin'!

Nothing but the Best for the New Baby. ("Glascock's Combination Baby Jumper" and Rocking Chair)

Expreßgut

NÜRNBERGER SPIELWAREN imported by the Bon Ton Store

Advents- u. Weihnachts-dekoration

Nähmaschine

BLACKSMITH

GRAN'PA'S HOUSE was on the edge of the Village

And there was a Hat Rack in the front hall (with a tray of calling cards) and the nicest, slipperiest, "sliding-down-banister" in town!

GRAN'MA

GRAN'PA

God bless our home

There was a hanging lamp in the parlor

And a bracket lamp over the kitchen sink, which had a pump!

And there was a shiny coal stove in the settin' room!

And what were once (alas!) the pride and joy of some proud peacock!

LM

THE PARLOR always smelled good with its Bay Window just full of geraniums

The Whatnot held just about everything from Agates (from way out West) to Zonite. (That came from Mt. Vesuvius)

And looking down on you every minute were the charcoal likenesses of Aunt Naomi

Besides being very ornamental(?) the fireplace was good for corn popping

There was a melodious hymnsing around the melodeon on Christmas Eve

And Uncle Azaria

(both long gone)

a whole BARREL of apples

In the cellar there was a cistern for hollering down into And back came echoes!

HELLO-O-ELLO-O

HELLO

THE whole family went to Yuletide service in the country church that papa and mamma attended in their younger days.

The children were intrigued by the "central heating" * and the interruptions caused by its appetite for wood

* (center of the Church, that is.)

The Pastor's Text was from Luke 2: 13-15 and his sermon: "Peace on Earth".

The children each received the Pastor's Christmas card and an Orange from the Sunday School Superintendent

Riding home in the moonlight behind his dappled grays, Uncle Alvin was SURE there was Peace on his part of the earth.

Now, the vacation was over, but not until the "Country Cousins" had agreed to spend NEXT Christmas with the "City Folks"

(Besides they had always wanted to go up on top of that 12 story "skyscraper" they had heard so much about!)

The children wanted them to see "how pretty" THEIR city church was at Christmastime!

And to take a ride in a trolley car

and maybe see a "RUN" by the Fire Engines!!

"Peace on the earth, good-will to men

HERE WE ARE at the end of our tour and we are back 'midst the hurry-scurry of our modern holiday season! And while some folks may have their doubts, WE think there's still a lot of "PEACE ON EARTH AMONG MEN OF GOOD WILL."

We drove to Nebraska every Christmas for many years, Mother and I, continuing a practice begun when I was a boy and my father was still alive. We stopped first in Omaha to spend a rather stiff, unfestive Christmas Eve with my father's family, the Edwardses, and then early the next morning went on to a ranch further west where we had a jolly time with my mother's people, the O'Kellys.

Not that the Edwardses were unkind or inhospitable. It's only that mother's relatives were much more spontaneous and high-spirited by nature. At Christmas dinner the O'Kellys specialized in stories so uproarious they must have been invented, although they often began or ended with the phrase, "Swear to God." And after dinner, even more aunts and uncles and cousins came pouring through the house to greet us. Any given Christmas, we probably saw 35 O'Kellys.

Christmas Eve in Omaha was observed with fewer people, and mostly without laughter. An Edwards conversation followed a predictable line, beginning with the unreliability of the weather and leading on through the deteriorating condition of their aging automobiles and their ailing friends and neighbors. As a young man I used to consider this talk painfully dull, but over the years I learned to take a certain pleasure in the constancy of it, the way you will sometimes come to appreciate a cheerless old hymn in church simply because it is so familiar. I suppose, as we age, any sign of permanence consoles us, no matter if it bores us besides.

I find it curious that despite the high colors of the O'Kelly Christmases, the Edwardses, as a family, are more clearly etched in my boyhood memories. Grandfather Edwards, a small man with a mustache and a hearing aid, was made to seem even smaller by the engulfing overstuffed chair he always sat in. "Come, Leland, we'll read," he used to declare, and I would climb up on his lap and be read to from a book of moralizing tales about a boy named Henry. I remember Grandmother Edwards setting seven places at the

My father's clear voice sang from the celluloid record, "I'll be home for Christmas."

CHRISTMAS EVE IN
Omaha

JON HASSLER

table, for we were always joined by Aunt Cora, Uncle Herbert, and their son Wesley, who lived nearby. Uncle Herbert was a butcher. Cousin Wesley was mischievous, and I never liked him very much. Grandmother would sit at the foot of the table, silently nibbling and smiling at me whenever our eyes met.

This smile, never quite joyous, turned very sad the year I was eight and my father was stationed in California and waiting to be shipped out to the war in the South Pacific. I recall the phonograph record he sent home to his parents that winter. Although he'd printed a message on the back of the envelope—"Don't open without Lolly and Leland present"—Cousin Wesley was discovered opening it before we got there. It was unlike any record we had ever seen—small, thin, bendable, and nearly transparent, with grooves only on one side. It had a red, white, and blue label on which was printed "U.S.O. San Francisco."

Grandfather set it on the spindle, lowered the needle, and we were all astonished to hear my father's voice. He was singing, a cappella, "I'll be home for Christmas." Mother laughed and wept. Grandmother only wept. I felt supremely triumphant, for not only did Wesley's father have no singing voice, he'd also been rejected as physically unfit for the armed forces. We played the record again and again, far into the night.

The following Christmas season, a glimmer of joy appeared in Grandmother Edwards' smile, for my father was safely home. But five years later—I was fourteen— the smile turned severely sad again, and stayed that way for the rest of her life. That was the year my father was killed by lightning while fishing from a canoe.

Of course Mother and I, too, were devastated. Over time, Mother gradually recovered, calling on inner resources I didn't seem to have. She began to laugh once more, and I resented her laughter. As an introspective and only child, I'd never found it easy to make friends, and so my father had been my closest chum. Fortunately, he'd left me a legacy of absorbing hobbies—fishing, stamp-collecting, playing the piano—and these I pursued with a kind of mad intensity; yet I could never quite throw off the gloom I felt

quired an affinity for—indeed, I found myself imitating—the Edwards' reticence, their measured, mournful ways. True, I still enjoyed Christmas Day on the O'Kelly ranch, but I found myself looking forward more eagerly to Christmas Eve in Omaha, where my father's memory was held in sacred trust.

When, with time, my memories of my father began to fade, my melancholy did not. It was compounded, in fact, by guilt. I wanted to be able to dwell on his life the way they did in Omaha. So intense was their devotion that I began to feel extremely unworthy. In retrospect, of course, I see that my common sense was telling me to quit probing my wound and get on with my life, but to do so at the time would have seemed a kind of betrayal. It took the upheaval of a moving day to shake me out of this state of unhealthy nostalgia.

I think it was my twenty-sixth Christmas when my grandparents decided to leave their house in Omaha and take a suburban apartment. In planning to be packed and moved by Christmas Eve, they'd overestimated not only their endurance but also the hours of help Cousin Wesley was to give them. And when Mother and I arrived around noon, we found Grandfather exhausted and deeply asleep in his overstuffed chair, Grandmother full of tearful apologies, and the house in disarray—curtains down, cupboards half empty, dozens of half-packed boxes scattered

whenever it occurred to me that I must go on living in a world bereft of my dear father.

Too bad that a tragedy of that magnitude was required to bring me into a closer union with my father's family, but that's what happened. I ac-

through the rooms. Soon Wesley arrived with his parents and his pickup, and we all pitched in, working far into the evening and getting about half their belongings moved into the apartment before all of us wore out.

Christmas Eve dinner was takeout Chinese, eaten around midnight. We were sipping coffee and munching Aunt Cora's holiday cookies, when I brought out the celluloid record of my father's voice. Earlier, while working with Grandmother in the attic, I'd come across it in a hatbox of mementos. I put it on the turntable. The sound was amazingly clear; his voice so wonderfully fresh and melodious that he seemed to be present in the room. "I'll be home for Christmas," he sang, and we sat there enchanted. I played it a second time, and we exchanged a few reverent remarks. I played it a third time, and each of us gazed off in a private direction, calling up private memories. Even Cousin Wesley seemed moved.

I switched it off then, and a curious conversation ensued. It began with Grandfather, who declared, "Typical of that boy not to say it right out that he was coming home."

"Yes, that was his sweet way," said Aunt Cora, concerning her brother. "Tell us in a song like that. And the next thing, there he was."

"Typical," Grandfather repeated, as though the memory irked him. "Surprise you like that. Never say it straight out."

Uncle Herbert agreed. "Just gave us that one clue."

"But he didn't. . ." began Grandmother, her memory evidently clearer than theirs, but she was not given a chance to finish. Aunt Cora was remembering the gifts he'd brought from Hawaii:

"To this day I keep the Pearl Harbor pillow on the daybed. And Wesley, don't you still carry that jackknife?"

Cousin Wesley said he did.

Aunt Cora turned to Mother. "Lolly, you must've been the most surprised of all when he showed up. You and Leland."

Mother and I exchanged a look, and before she could point out that they had their Christmas memories mixed up, Aunt Cora was going on: "Or did you and Leland know ahead of time and not tell us?"

"Seems like yesterday," said Uncle Herbert.

"I thought he'd be in uniform, but he wasn't," said Wesley.

Grandmother timidly made another attempt. "I don't think he came home that Christmas. . . ."

And Mother came to her aid. "It was the following year he brought the things from Hawaii."

Grandfather declared both of them mistaken. First the record appeared, then my father himself, the same day. Wesley and his parents all nodded their support.

"Oh, so that's how it was," said Grandmother, and I watched a smile spread across her face as she allowed herself to believe this erroneous version. It made such a pleasing story after all.

I spoke up then, pointing out that the song wasn't about actually coming home for Christmas—only dreaming about it.

Mother, too, persisted, repeating the facts—the record one Christmas, his homecoming the next. None of this made an impression on them. With Grandmother forsaking the truth and going over to the other side, we were outnumbered five to two. There was a moment or two of strain—a kind of silent standoff—before Mother laughed and said, "What difference does it make? At least we have his voice. Would you play it again, Leland?"

And so we listened once more, all of us sitting there in a kind of stupor of satisfaction: Grandfather, Aunt Cora, Uncle Herbert, and Wesley happily picturing the day they'd invented; Grandmother putting their invention together, piece by piece, in her imagination; Mother not caring what they thought, only relishing in the sound of the voice preserved so fortuitously by the U.S.O., San Francisco.

And I, of course, was relieved beyond measure as I watched a pleasing myth replace the less dramatic facts, and I saw how trivial were the memories I'd been trying so hard to preserve.

Memories, fading and flawed, were all they had in Omaha, while I had my father's fishing tackle, his stamp collection, his sheet music. Like him, I was a school teacher. I lived in his house. I had his knack for catching walleyes. I didn't have his singing voice, but I had his talent at the piano. I had his way of walking, said Mother, with my left foot slightly splayed. I knew from photographs that I had his forehead and eyes. And I had this family of his, who, I sensed, would go on worshiping his memory over the years, preserving it, in their way, from oblivion, while I went ahead and lived the life he lost.

MY CHRISTMAS
Classic

My favorite memories of Christmas include: